HarperCollins books may be purchased for educational, business, or sales promotional use. For information, please write: Special Markets Department, HarperCollins Publishers, 10 East 53rd Street, New York, NY 10022.

First published in 2011 by Alfred A. Knopf Canada, a division of Random House of Canada Limited.

FIRST U.S. EDITION

Library of Congress Cataloging-in-Publication Data

Toews, Miriam.
Irma Voth : a novel / by Miriam Toews.
p. cm.
ISBN 978-0-06-207018-0
1. Young women—Mexico—Fiction. 2. Mennonites—Mexico—Fiction. 3. Families—Mexico—Fiction. 4. Self-actualization (Psychology) in women—Fiction. I. Title.
PR9199.3.T6113I76 2011
813'.54—dc22

2011008226

11 12 13 14 15 OFF/RRD 10 9 8 7 6 5 4 3 2 1

IRMA VOTH

A Novel

MIRIAM TOEWS

HARPER
An Imprint of HarperCollins*Publishers*
www.harpercollins.com

ALSO BY MIRIAM TOEWS

FICTION

Summer of My Amazing Luck

A Boy of Good Breeding

A Complicated Kindness

The Flying Troutmans

MEMOIR

Swing Low: A Life

IRMA VOTH

for my mother, Elvira

IRMA VOTH

ONE

JORGE SAID HE WASN'T COMING BACK until I learned how to be a better wife. He said it's okay to touch him with my arm or my leg or my foot, if it's clean, when we're sleeping but not to smother him like a second skin. I asked him how could that be, I hardly saw him any more and he said that's a good thing for you. He said people always lie about their reasons for leaving and what difference does it make?

I blocked the doorway so he wouldn't leave and I begged him not to go. He put his hands on my shoulders and then he rubbed my arms like he was trying to warm me up and I put my hands on his waist.

I asked him how I was supposed to develop the skills to be a wife if I didn't have a husband to practise with and he said that was the type of question that contributed to my loneliness. I asked him why he was trying to blindside me with answers that attempted only to categorize my questions and I asked him why he was acting so strange lately and where his problem with the way I slept with my leg over his leg had come from and why he kept going away and why he was trying so hard to be a tough guy instead of just Jorge and then he pulled me close to him and he asked me to please stop talking, to stop shivering, to stop blocking the door, to stop crying and to stop loving him.

I asked him how I was supposed to do that and he said no, Irma, we're not kids anymore, don't say anything else. I wanted to ask him what loving him had to do with being childish but I did what he told me to do and I kept my mouth shut. He looked so sad, his eyes were empty, they were half closed, and he kissed me and he left. But before he drove off he gave me a new flashlight with triple C batteries and I'm grateful for it because this is a very dark, pitch-black part of the world.

The first time I met Jorge was at the rodeo in Rubio. He wasn't a cowboy or a roper, he was just a guy watching in the stands. We weren't allowed to go to rodeos normally but my father was away from home, visiting another colony in Belize, and my mother told my sister Aggie and me that we could take the truck and go to the rodeo for the day if we took the boys with us so she could rest. She might have been pregnant. Or maybe she had just lost the baby. I'm not sure. But she didn't care about rules that afternoon so, miraculously, we found ourselves at a rodeo. Maybe it was the pure adrenalin rush of being away from the farm that made me feel bold but I noticed Jorge sitting there by himself, watching intently, and kind of moving his body subtly in a way that matched the movements of the real cowboys, and I thought it was funny, and so I decided to go up to him and say hello.

Are you pretending to be a cowboy? I asked him in Spanish.

He smiled, he was a little embarrassed, I think.

Are you pretending to be a Mennonitzcha? he said.

No, I really am, I said.

He asked me if I wanted to sit next to him and I said yes, but only for a minute because I had to get back to Aggie and the boys.

We had a conversation in broken English and Spanish but it wasn't much of one because as soon as I sat down beside him my boldness evaporated and my knees started to shake from nervousness. I was worried that somebody would see me talking to a Mexican boy and tell my father. Jorge told me he was in town buying something, I can't remember what, for his mother who lived in Chihuahua city. He told me that he had a job delivering cars over the U.S. border from Juárez to El Paso and that he got paid forty American dollars a car and he didn't ask questions.

Questions about what? I asked him.

Anything, he said.

But about what? I said.

About what's in the cars or who's paying me or when or just anything. I don't ask, he said. He seemed a little nervous, so we both looked around at the people in the stands for a minute without saying much.

Some people are staring at us, he said.

No they're not, I said.

Well, actually they are. Look at that guy over there. He was about to lift his arm and point but I said no, please, don't.

He told me he thought it was strange that a Mennonite girl was at a rodeo and I told him that yeah it was. I tried to explain the rules my father had but that he was out of town and my mother was tired and all that and then we started talking about mothers and fathers and eventually he told me this story about his dad.

All I really understood was that his father had left his mother when he was a little boy and that one day his mother had told him he was going to meet him for the first time and he better look sharp and behave himself. She said she was going to drop him off on this corner by their house and his dad would be there waiting for him and then they could have a conversation, maybe get a meal together, and then the dad would drop him back off on that corner when they were done. So Jorge, he was five years old, decided he had better clean up his sneakers, especially if he wanted to look sharp for his dad. He washed them in the bathtub with shampoo and then he put them in the sun to dry. When it was time to go, his mom dropped him off at the corner and said goodbye and left and Jorge stood there for a long time, waiting. The sky got darker and darker. Finally it started to rain and Jorge started to worry. Where was his dad? Some men in cars drove past him but nobody stopped to pick him up. It started to rain harder. Then Jorge looked down at his shoes and noticed that they were foaming. Bubbles were floating around by his shoes and he didn't know what was going on. He was too young to understand that he hadn't rinsed his sneakers when he washed them with shampoo and now the rain was rinsing them for him and the soap was bubbling out of them and making them foam. Jorge felt like a fool. Like a clown. He was mortified. He was just about to take them off and rub them in the dirt on the sidewalk to try to make them stop foaming when a car pulled up and a man got out and introduced himself to Jorge as his father. He asked Jorge what was going on with his sneakers and Jorge told him that he didn't know. That they had just strangely started foaming like that and his father looked at him and told him that shoes didn't normally do that. Jorge had wanted to tell him that he had only been trying to look good and clean for his dad but he didn't really know how to say that and so he just started crying out of shame.

And then what happened? I asked Jorge.

My father told me that he loved my shoes that way, that they were great, that he wanted a pair just like them, said Jorge. That made me feel a lot better. And then we went and had some shrimp cocktail. Afterwards he dropped me back off at the corner and I never saw him again.

Oh, I said. Where did he go?

I don't know, said Jorge. But I was sure it was because of my stupid shoes that he never came back. I realized that he had lied to me. Obviously he didn't want a pair of shoes that foamed up. Who would want that? So eventually I made this decision not to act like an idiot in life.

But you weren't trying to be a clown, I said. You just wanted to have clean shoes to meet your dad. Your mom had told you to.

I know, he said, maybe it's not rational. But after that I decided I would try to be a cooler boy and not try so hard for things.

I told Jorge that I was sorry about that but that I had to get back to Aggie and the boys.

I guess I'll never see you again either, he said. He was smiling. He told me it was nice meeting me and I said he could visit me in our field, maybe, beside the broken crop-duster that had crashed in it, and I gave him directions and told him to wait there later that evening.

Make sure you look sharp and behave yourself, I told him. But I didn't really say it correctly in Spanish so he didn't get the little joke which wasn't funny anyway and he just nodded and said he'd wait all night and all year if he had to. And I wasn't used to that kind of romantic speaking so I said no, it wouldn't take that long. I wanted to tell him that I had tried most of my life to do things that would make people stay too, and that none of them had worked out, but then I thought that if I said that our relationship would always be defined by failure.

Jorge came to visit me a few times, secretly, on his way between El Paso and Chihuahua city. We would lie in the back of his truck and count the number of seconds it took for jet streams to evaporate. If you happened to fly over this place you'd see three houses in a row and nothing else for miles but cornfields and desert. Mine and Jorge's in the middle and on one side of us my parents' house and on the other side an empty house where my cousins used to live, the space between them approximately the size of a soccer pitch or a cemetery. On a clear day I can see the Sierra Madre mountains way off in the west, and sometimes I talk to them. I compliment them on their strength and solidity, and by hearing myself talk that way I am reminded that those words exist for a reason, that they're applicable from time to time. It's comforting. There are a few little villages around here. Some are Mexican and some are Mennonite, we're sorted like buttons, and we're expected to stay where we're put.

If Jorge visited in the evening he and I would lie in the back of his truck and stare at the stars and trace the shapes of various constellations and touch each other's bodies very gently like we were burn victims. Jorge told me that I didn't have to be so nervous. Don't you want to leave this place? he said.

I think so, I said.

So even if your father finds out about us the worst thing that can happen is we go away.

I know, but, I said. But then we can't come back, really.

So, he said. Why would you want to?

Well, I said. I would miss my mother and my sister and—

But Irma, he said, you could visit them secretly just like what we're doing right now.

I don't know, I said.

But you and I are in love, he said. We're eighteen now. We don't need our mothers so much.

He told me that it was like a star museum out here, there were so many of them, every different kind from all the ages, stored right here in my campo for safekeeping. He said I could be the curator of the star museum.

I'd rather not.

I was just saying stuff.

I know, I said, but I'm not good at keeping things safe.

I know, he said, I didn't mean it for real, it was just a thing to say.

I know, I said, but I can't be the curator of anything.

Okay, Irma. I understand. You don't have to take care of the stars, okay? That was just stuff to say. It was stupid.

I had meant to tell him, again, that I wasn't good at keeping promises or secrets or people from leaving. I kept meaning to tell Jorge things.

On our wedding day nobody came except the justice of the peace from the Registro Civil in Cuauhtémoc, who finished the ceremony in under a minute. He got lost trying to follow Jorge's directions to our campo and it was dark by the time he finally showed up. Jorge had brought a candle with him and he lit it and put it next to the piece of paper we had to sign and when I leaned over to write my name, Irma Voth, my veil caught on fire and Jorge pulled it off my head and threw it onto the ground and stomped the fire out. We were in a sheltered grove near my parents' farm. The justice of the peace told me I was a lucky girl and Jorge grabbed my hand and we took off, running. He wore a white shirt that was too big on him and hard plastic shoes. We didn't really know what to do but after a while we stopped running and we walked around for a long time and then we went to my house and told my parents that we had got married and my mother went to her bedroom and closed the door softly and my father slapped me in the face. Jorge pinned him to the wall of the kitchen and said he'd kill him if he did it again. I went into my mother's bedroom and we hugged each other and she asked me if I loved Jorge. I said yes. I told her that he and I were going to go to Chihuahua city now and that we would live with his mother for a while until we found jobs and our own place to live. Then my father came into the room and told me that Jorge and I weren't going anywhere, that we were going to live in the house next door and work for him and that if we didn't he'd turn Jorge over to the cops and that the cops would sooner put a bullet in the head of another greasy narco than bother with the paperwork of processing him. He didn't say it in a fierce or menacing way, just in a way that made it clear and final. And then he left the house and my mother went into the kitchen and put some buns and cheese onto the table and a rhubarb *platz* that she cut up into small pieces. Jorge and I sat down with her, on either side, and she held our hands and prayed for our happiness and for an everlasting love. She spoke quietly so the other kids wouldn't wake up. After that she whispered congratulations to us in Low

German and I told Jorge what she had said and they smiled at each other, I had forgotten how pretty her smile was. Jorge thanked her for the gift of me and she asked him to protect and cherish that gift. Then my father came back into the house and told us to get out and that we were no longer welcome in his home. Jorge and I walked down the road to our house and he took my hand and asked me if I believed what the justice of the peace had said, that I was a lucky girl. I looked west towards the Sierra Madre mountains but I couldn't make them out in the darkness. Jorge's hand was a little sweaty and I squeezed it and he was kind enough to let that be my answer.

We lived in the house for free but worked for my father for nothing. We looked after the cows so that he could work the fields and travel around from campo to campo imploring people to continue with old traditions even though the drought was killing us. The plan was that when my little brothers were older they would help him with the farm, and Jorge and I would be booted out of the house. Jorge said he wasn't worried about that because he had other opportunities to make money and eventually he and I could follow our dream of living in a lighthouse. We didn't know of one but he said he knew people in the Yucatán who would help us. I didn't even really know exactly where the ocean was.

But none of that actually matters now and it's embarrassing to talk about because Jorge is gone and I'm still here and there's no lighthouse on my horizon as far as I can see.

Jorge came and went all that year and I never knew when he'd show up but when he did it wasn't for long so I really saw no one, except the cows.

One morning my little sister Aggie snuck over and gave me some news. She told me that filmmakers from Mexico City were moving into the empty house next to mine and our father said she wasn't supposed to talk to them or in any way whatsoever to acknowledge them.

She also told me that she had a new dream of becoming a singer of canciones rancheras, which are ballads of love and infidelity and drunken husbands. She had new dreams every day.

I missed Aggie. I missed her big laugh and her little tricks. I missed listening to her practice her swearing deep under the blankets so our parents wouldn't hear. She has white-blond hair and a brown face from the sun and blue eyes that are so light they're almost translucent, like a wolf. She told me that the sun and the moon are the two eyes of God and when one disappears the other one pops up to keep spying on us. When we can see them both at the same time we're in big trouble and all we can do is run. Since I married Jorge she hadn't been allowed to talk to me, which is why she had to sneak over, but it wasn't really sneaking, not entirely, because our mother usually knew when she was coming and sometimes sent things along.

According to my father, Jorge was more interested in searching for sensations in Chihuahua city than taking care of the cows and the corn in Campo 6.5. He had other reasons for not liking Jorge but the real reason was that I'd married a non-Mennonite. A long time ago, in the twenties, seven Mennonite men travelled from Manitoba to the Presidential Palace in Mexico City to make a deal. They'd been offered this land for cheap and they decided to accept the offer and move everyone from their colony in central Canada down to Mexico where they wouldn't have to send their kids to regular school or teach them to speak English or dress them in normal clothing. Mennonites formed themselves in Holland five hundred years ago after a man named Menno Simons became so moved by hearing Anabaptist prisoners singing hymns before being executed by the Spanish Inquisition that he joined their cause and became their leader. Then they started to move all around the world in colonies looking for freedom and isolation and peace and opportunities to sell cheese. Different countries give us shelter if we agree to stay out of trouble and help with the economy by farming in obscurity. We live like ghosts. Then, sometimes, those countries decide they want us to be real citizens after all and start to force us to do things like join the army or pay taxes or respect laws and then we pack our stuff up in the middle of the night and move to another country where we can live purely but somewhat out of context. Our motto is from the "rebuke of wordliness," which is from the Biblical book of James: *Whosoever will be a friend of the world is the enemy of God.*

I once made the mistake of asking my father if it didn't make sense that in all those years from then to now some Mennonite girl would fall for a Mexican boy and want to marry him. It's called integration, Dad, it's not a big deal.

I mean if you accept their cheap offer of land . . . But he had stopped listening to me ages ago. The last real thing we talked about was the absurdity of life on earth. He was thinking about something he'd read in an old newspaper that had somehow managed to float into our field from El Paso or somewhere. We were in the truck on our way to Cuauhtémoc and he asked me how I thought it was possible that a crowd of people could stand on the street in front of a tall office building and cheer a suicidal man on to his death by encouraging him to jump. I was surprised by the question and said I didn't know. What does that say about us? said my dad. That we're cruel, I said. Then my dad said no, he didn't think so, he thought it meant that we feel mocked, that we feel and appear stupid and cowardly in the presence of this suicidal man who has wisely concluded that life on earth is ridiculous. And we want him to die immediately so that the pain of being confronted with our own fear and ignorance will also, mercifully, end. Would you agree with that? my dad asked. What? I said. I didn't know what he was asking me. It's a sin to commit suicide, I thought. I said no, I still think it means we're cruel. My dad said no, it doesn't mean we're cruel. He got a little mad at me and stopped talking to me for a while and then as time passed never got back into the habit.

My father had lost his family when he was a little kid, when they'd been driven off their farm near the Black Sea. His parents and his sisters had been slaughtered by soldiers on a road somewhere in Russia, beside trees, and buried quickly in the ditch. My father survived by singing some songs, German hymns I think, for the soldiers, who thought it was cute, this little blond boy, but eventually the novelty of that wore off and they foisted him onto some other fleeing Mennonite family who adopted him and brought him to Canada to help with the animals and baling. He hated his adopted family and ran away when he was twelve to work on some other farm where he met my mother and eventually married her. That's all I know about that because by the time it occurred to me to ask him questions about it he had stopped talking to me. I tried to get more details from my mother but she said she didn't know any more than that either.

We'd had fun, me and him, you know, typical farm fun, when I was young. He made me a swing that I could jump from into hay and he understood my grief when my favourite chicken died. He even brought me to the fabric store to buy some flannel to make a burial suit of little trousers and a vest and hat for my chicken and he let me bury it outside my bedroom window rather than tossing it into the rubble fire like the other dead ones. But it was colossal and swift like the sinking of the *Titanic* the way all that disappeared when he moved us overnight to Mexico.

Two weeks after we moved here my mother took me to the doctor for the first time in Cuauhtémoc and told him that I thought I was dead and nothing she or my father said could convince me of the truth. I was thirteen years old, the same age that Aggie is now. My father stayed outside in the truck. The doctor spoke to me in Spanish and I didn't understand him very well. His office was in a big barn and the nurse was his wife. He had a small revolver in his pocket but before he examined me he took it out and laid it on his desk. He asked me what my life was like when I was alive.

I don't know, I said.

Is this your life after death? he asked me.

Yes, I said. I think so.

How did you die? he asked.

I don't know, I said.

Food poisoning? he asked.

Maybe, I said. I don't know.

Snake bite? he said.

No, I said.

Heart attack?

I'm not sure.

Do you feel that you were born and lived and then you died or that you have never lived at all? he asked.

I was born and lived and then died, I said.

So, he said, do you think that you're in heaven?

I don't know, I said.

What makes you feel like you're dead? he said. Are you numb in some parts of your body?

No, I said. I don't know.

Did you see yourself die? he asked.

Yes, I said.

How did you die? he asked.

I'm not sure, I said.

But you saw yourself die? he said.

Yes, I said.

In a dream? he said.

I don't know, I said.

If you still feel that you are dead in six weeks will you please come back to see me? he said.

I looked at my mother and she nodded. She didn't like his question about food poisoning. The doctor thanked her for bringing me to see him and patted her arm. He put his pistol back into his pocket. My father was still sitting in the truck, waiting for us. He asked my mother if I still thought I was dead.

I don't know, she said.

Why is it so important to you whether I'm alive or not? I asked them.

It's not whether you're alive or not, said my father. Clearly you're alive. It's what you believe. He pinched my arm. Do you feel that?

I nodded.

You need to stop playing games, Irma Voth, he said.

Someday you'll be a wife and mother, Irma, said my own mother. Will you come alive for that? I didn't know what to tell her. How was I supposed to know? On the way home I put my head in her lap and she undid my braids and combed my hair with her fingers. I like to remember how that felt. She was so gentle. I still don't understand how she managed to take out my tight braids without any tugging or pain. Irma, she whispered to me, just begin. I didn't know what she meant. When we got back she stayed with me in my bed even though I was thirteen and rubbed circles on my back slowly.

Aggie and I sat on the fence and talked. We were surrounded by nothing but three farmhouses in a neat row, sky and corn. How are the boys? I asked.

Annoying, she said. We had two little brothers, Doft and Jacobo, who liked to connect everything with rope.

Are they still tying shit together? I asked.

Yeah, and hiding shoes, she said. She told me that already my father was fighting with the director of the movie.

He's here now? I said.

He came early, said Aggie. Mom and I listened to him talking with Dad in the kitchen. Dad said he'd shoot his dog if it attacks the cows or even if he sees him in the cornfields. He's a fighting pit bull from Mexico City, Irma, and the director said he's got a haunted soul and a natural sweetness, and he'll play in the movie as a dog of the family. Dad told him that no family here has a fighting dog from Mexico City and especially not one with a soul and that's the first sign the director doesn't know what he's doing.

Aggie told me the director said he had invested almost all of his own money into his art, into making this film about beautiful people in a beautiful part of the world, and that he has nothing but respect and admiration for the Mennonites. My father asked the director if the dog was really there purely for protection. He accused the director of lying to him. That the dog was there to protect his expensive camera equipment. The director denied that and said no, the dog would be an integral part of the film. Aggie said that our father told the director that films were like beautiful cakes, filled with shit.

How can he say that when he's never seen them? I asked her.

He says art is a lie, said Aggie.

We sat on the fence and stared at things. Artless things. Things that were true. Things that belonged to ourselves and to each other. The clouds, our clothing, my hands. A bird flying over us had two long twigs in its mouth and he dropped one so that it landed directly at our feet like it was a gift. Here you go, Mennonite girls, prepare a nest. Or maybe it was an attack.

Dad says you believe in God but not an afterlife, said Aggie. He says that's impossible.

That's not remotely accurate, I told her. I never said that.

Frieda's dad drove his truck the wrong way down the highway to Cuauhtémoc, said Aggie.

What a moron, I said.

No, she said, he killed himself.

On purpose? I said.

I don't know, said Aggie. Didn't he drive there all the time? Did they secretly reverse the directions?

What are they gonna do? I said.

Who knows, said Aggie. Get a new truck? Katharina at school said he owed money to narcos.

Aggie, I said.

Well, how should I know? she said. Oh, I have this for you. She pulled a tiny infant's undershirt out of her pocket. There was a small faded flower on the collar. You wore it in

Canada if you were a baby, she said. Mom told me to give it to you.

Thanks, I said. *When* I was a baby.

When you were a baby? said Aggie. English is such a prick.

You're pretty good at it, I said.

Oh, and this is from her too, she said, and kissed me on the cheek.

Get lost, I said.

Can I come live with you, Irma? said Aggie.

Well, I said, are you looking for a quick and easy way to complicate your life forever?

Maybe I could live with you secretly, she said.

We sat quietly. We heard cows practising their English, trying with no luck to form words.

What's he trying to say? said Aggie.

Help, I said. Our own stupid joke.

I told her to go before it got so dark she'd fall into the ditch on her way home but she didn't move. Aggie ignores all my advice, as though she were determined to live successfully, and we sat on the fence for a long time. Then we started to get stiff from sitting and began to kick each other lightly in the dark.

When are they moving in? I asked Aggie.

I don't know, she said. Tonight.

My power was still off and I couldn't find the flashlight that Jorge had given me. I thought about bringing a cow into the house for company, just one. A small one. Or I could sleep in the barn like Jesus but without the entourage or the pressure to perform. I lay in my bed thinking of ways I could make Jorge happy if he ever came home again. One was: wash my feet before going to bed and dry them completely. The other one was: be hotter. It was true, what Jorge had said, that we weren't kids anymore. I loved chasing him around fields and having dried turd fights and hiding in the corn while he looked for me and planning our future together in the Yucatán in a lighthouse with round rooms and a pole in the middle that we would use to slide down from the top floor directly into a boat that with one shove would put us out to sea. I told him we could call the boat Katie but he said he'd have to name it after his mother and even that was okay with me, I didn't argue. I knew I would be alone for the rest of my life if Jorge didn't come back to me. No boy from any of the Mennonite colonies would want a woman who'd been married and abandoned and especially one who'd been married to a Mexican.

I decided to go out and spy on my family from the roof of their grain shed. I could see directly into their large room. I thought about throwing myself off the roof of the grain shed and onto the roof of the outdoor kitchen which they're not using now and lying there, dead, for months, invisible but toxic.

I wondered how long it would take them to find me. Then I remembered that they wouldn't be looking. Well, maybe Aggie would be looking, but that's the thing that stopped me from doing it. I had one question of myself: how do I preserve my dignity when nobody else is watching? By believing in a happy ending, I told myself. I had to get out of the house.

I stood in my yard and noticed the lights on at my cousins' old place. The filmmakers had arrived. And then I heard voices and music and laughter and I had never felt more alone and strange in my life, which is something. I went back into my house and lay in my bed some more and tried to pray. God, I said, help me to live. Help me to live, please. Please God, help me to live. God, I need your help. I need to live. Please? I need help living. God. Help. I had never learned how to pray properly. It didn't make sense that God would require me to articulate my pain in order for him to feel it and respond. I wanted to negotiate a deal. I knew I wasn't supposed to talk to the filmmakers but wondered if it would be acceptable to observe them from a distance. I punched myself on the side of my head. What difference did it make what my father had said? I posed another question to myself. How do I behave in this world without following the directions of my father, my husband or God? Does it all end with me sleeping in a barn with cows and creeping around the campo spying on people from the roofs of empty grain sheds?

I got up again and went outside and crept along in the darkness towards the filmmakers' house. I leaned against the water pump in the side yard and watched while several guys unloaded a million black boxes from a truck and a car and a van and carried them into the house. All the lights were on and the filmmakers were laughing and talking loudly and music was playing from somewhere inside. A dog was barking. In fact, a dog was barking and running at me in the dark and it looked like his eyes were on fire and I could see sparks flying out of them. I thought, well, I should run now, but I couldn't move, I was galvanized to the pump, and then I heard a man yell, Oveja, Oveja!

Which is how I met Diego, the director of the film.

Vive aquí? he said. He was kneeling, looking up at me, and holding on to Oveja's collar.

No, I said. Well, yes. Over there. I pointed. I tried to smile. I shook with fear. I may have bitten off a piece of my own tongue.

Me llamo Diego, said Diego.

Irma, I said.

Mucho gusto, Irma.

Mucho gusto.

Diego released Oveja and the dog wandered back to the house and Diego and I stood in the dark by the pump. He spoke quickly and precisely but his voice was soft, as though he were helping me through an emergency. He told me that Oveja, the pit bull, used to be a champion fighter in Guadalajara. He told me that Oveja, like every living thing, needs to love and be loved. And that his eyes tell a story of pain and suffering, and that he is haunted by his criminal past, a life he would never have chosen for himself.

Oveja and I are blood brothers, Diego said. We were

soldiers and now we are artists. He explained that before he became a filmmaker he was involved in armed conflict, though on the legal end of things.

Oveja will eventually play the part of the family dog in my movie, said Diego.

I know, I said.

Ah, you do? he asked.

He suggested that we move closer to the yard light so that we could see each other's faces. He smiled and I looked at him closely. He wore a thin thread around his neck and attached to the thread was a small piece of paper the size of a postage stamp. It had writing on it but I couldn't read it. He had a red dot in the white part of his left eye, like a tiny pilot light.

Which languages do you speak, Irma? he asked me.

German, Spanish and English, I said.

Do you want a job? he asked me.

I don't know, I said. I think I have one.

What is it? he said.

The farm, I said. I glanced over at the barn behind my house. And . . . wife.

How old are you, Irma?

I'm nineteen years old, I said.

And you're married? he said.

Yes, I said, for one year already.

Have you been here all your life?

I was born in Canada, I said.

Where is your husband? he said.

He's in the city.

Which city?

Chihuahua. Or Juárez.

For how long?

I don't know.

Would you like to make some extra money as a translator? he said.

Diego said he'd explain to me in Spanish or English what he wanted his German actress to say and do and I'd tell her, in German, what it was. He told me that it didn't really matter what the actors were saying because nobody watching the film would understand the language anyway. It wasn't really German that they'd be speaking, it was Low German, which is the unwritten language of the Mennonite people and hardly used in the world anymore. And besides, he said, there will be subtitles.

My actors could be saying I have worms, you have worms, we all have worms, he said, and nobody would know the difference. Do you understand, Irma?

I do, I said.

But I want *them* to know what they're saying, he said. So that they'll feel the words and produce the appropriate emotional response.

He told me that Miguel, a sixteen-year-old production assistant, will pick Marijke the German actress up at the airport in Chihuahua city tomorrow and bring her here to Campo 6.5 and we'll begin to shoot the movie the next day after she's had some time to rest.

I'm looking for internal energy and presence, Diego told me. I travelled around the world searching for the woman who would play this role. I want her to be beautiful, but not beautiful.

I understand, I told him.

I want her face to feel at home on an ancient coin, he said. I want her eyes to harm me. I want her, I mean *her*, to be too big for her body, a living secret, so that she is squeezed out through here, he said. He touched my forehead.

And here too, he said. He put his hand on my throat. And here, especially. He covered my eyes for a second.

And you found her? I said.

Yes, he said. In Germany. In a very small village. There was a woman in France but she was too beautiful.

Are you from Mexico City? I asked him.

Yes, but I've been living in Europe for the last few years. How long have you been living here? he asked me.

We came six years ago, I said.

It's very beautiful, he said.

It is? I said.

Yes, it's astonishing, he said.

What's Mexico City like? I said.

Ah, it's heaven and hell, he said. Are you nervous? You're shaking.

No, I said. I'm cold.

Why don't you come inside and meet the crew? he said. It's warm in there. I'll make you an espresso.

No, I have to get back to . . . there, I said. I pointed behind me.

The cornfield? he said.

I pointed again, towards the shadowy assortment of metal and concrete that housed my belongings. Diego smiled but I couldn't tell if he was sad or happy because he hadn't stopped smiling since rescuing me from his blood brother.

Okay, he said. But, quickly, let me just explain a few things to you about the job. We have a small crew, he said, and we are investing in time, not equipment and salaries. We all have specific responsibilities but everybody will be required to help out with everything. It's very necessary. Do you agree with that, Irma?

Sure, I said.

I hate stories and photographs, he said. They scare me. They freak me out. They're dead. I want emotion, the feeling, the emotional resonance of the person, the character coming out of a shot, a painting. I hate narrative. I hate actors. It's very important that your translation of my words is precise. Will it be?

Yes, I said.

And Irma, do you feel that we can rebel?

I don't know, I said. I had no idea what he was referring to, or on which word of the question to put the emphasis.

Do you feel that we can rebel against our oppressors without losing our love, our tolerance and our ability to forgive?

I don't know, I said. I looked around towards nature for a clue. A bird, a gust of wind, a star? But there was nothing, as though nature had noticed me trying to cheat and quickly covered up her answers. Diego put his hand on my shoulder and continued to smile.

Perfect, he said. You will be perfect.

———

The next morning Aggie and I met on the road between our houses and had one of our speed conversations. It's a silly thing we do together to make it seem like our imposed separation is not the source of continuous heartbreak and an abomination of what is just and loving but one long ridiculous joke like the Berlin Wall.

You're working for the filmmakers as a translator? That's crazy! Dad'll kill you! He already hates them!

I know, I said, so don't tell him. Diego will pay me and then I can use the money to go to Chihuahua or Juárez to find Jorge. Here, I have something for you.

What is it?

A switchblade. I brought it from Canada. Open it.

It's a comb!

It's a joke!

Drag.

Okay, then give it back to me!

No, I'll keep it.

I gotta go or you'll be in deep shit.

Irma, she said. But I had started to walk away. I heard her say some more things but by then I had yanked my skirt up and was running down the road away from her and begging the wind to obliterate her voice. She wanted to live with me. She missed me. She wanted me to come back home. She wanted to run away. She was yelling all this stuff and I wanted so badly for her to shut up. She was quiet for a second and I stopped running and turned around once to look at her. She was a thimble-sized girl on the road, a speck of a living thing. Her white-blond hair flew around her head like a small fire and it was all I could see because everything else about her blended in with the countryside.

He offered you a what? she yelled.

An espresso! I yelled back. It was like yelling at a shorting wire or a burning bush.

What is it? she said.

Coffee! I yelled.

Irma, can I come and live—

I turned around again and began to run.

TWO

I SPENT THE REST OF THE DAY cleaning the house and milking the cows and embroidering dangerous words onto the inside of my dresses, words like *lust* and *agony* and *Jorge*, and baking bread and yanking vegetables out of the ground, and making apple sauce with the apples that my aunt from Campo 4 had left for me at the end of the driveway with a note that said even sinners need to eat and a religious magazine with a headline that read the only way to heaven is to admit that you are a complete failure, and washing the windows and burning stuff and poisoning snake nests and killing rats. I didn't see Aggie for the rest of the day. I knew she was mad at me. I could picture her stomping around the house and being sassy to everyone and brandishing her useless weapon.

That night I took off all my clothes and examined my body. I had forgotten about it. I poked at it like a doctor would and asked myself did I feel this and did I feel that? Then I looked at my face in a small mirror and tried to make the two vertical lines between my eyebrows disappear by stretching the skin away on either side. I brushed my hair until my arms ached and then I draped it over my breasts like Eve when she was being flirty in the Garden.

I still had no power. I couldn't find the flashlight. The silver eye of God was right outside my bedroom window. I heard music coming from the filmmakers' house, by now Marijke the German actress would have arrived, and I fell asleep alone and naked in my bed.

The next morning there was a knock on my door. It was a boy wearing narrow black jeans and enormous white sneakers. He said he was Miguel, Diego's assistant, and I should come to the house immediately. Diego needed to explain things to Marijke before they began shooting and he needed me to help him do that. Miguel was very polite. When you are ready, he said. I told him I had to milk the cows first and he frowned. He asked me if he could help because Diego was already vibrating and we needed to hurry. There are sparks flying off him in every direction, he said.

What's that? I asked him. He was holding something in his hand.

A two-way radio, he said. Listen. He pushed a button on the radio. He put his finger to his lips.

We heard voices, one in particular.

Who's that? I said.

It's Diego, said Miguel. He pointed at the filmmakers' house.

Is he angry? I asked.

No, said Miguel, it's a motivational speech.

I told Miguel I'd do my milking fast but alone and be at the house in half an hour. I told him that if Diego needed to tell me things before that he could come see me in the barn and talk while I milked. He could bring Marijke if he wanted to.

Roger, said Miguel. Is that how you say that?

Roger? I asked.

Yeah, in Canada. They said you were from Canada?

I left when I was thirteen, I said. Maybe over and out?

Over and out, Irma, said Miguel.

Okay, I said.

Miguel took off and I stood in the sunshine for a couple of warm seconds trying to think of other coded ways to say yes, I understand, goodbye.

Half an hour later I averted another attack from Oveja by befriending him with wieners and applesauce. For a soldier turned artist he was still surprisingly aggressive.

The filmmakers had tied plastic bags filled with water all around the front porch of their house to keep the flies away. The bags of water sparkled in the sunlight like little chandeliers. I stood outside the door poised to knock while Oveja lay on the ground beside me devouring my leftovers. Then the door opened on its own, well, not on its own but from the inside and all the shouting stopped and Diego came over and kissed my cheek and took me into the huge kitchen to meet the crew.

The house that used to belong to my shy farmer cousins was now inhabited by tattooed artists who lay around smoking and drinking espresso and arguing about politics and camera angles. Diego asked me if I liked the music. I nodded. Have you heard of Tuberculosis? he asked. I nodded again. They're my favourite band, he said.

One by one they all got up and kissed me on the cheek and introduced themselves to me in Spanish or English or both. I didn't see Miguel anywhere. Diego explained to me each of their responsibilities. The camera, the sound, other things I had never heard of. We are creating a small world, he said. A world that is more real than the one we know. He told me that he had just discovered that a very important piece of the camera was missing. Show me your thumb, he said. I held it out to him. It's this small, he said. But it's the difference between life and death. Can you do your farm work without your thumb? he asked me. I shook my head. I thought of how annoyed Jorge would be if I lost my thumbs. Diego told me that two of the filmmakers, including Miguel, had driven to El Paso to pick up a replacement part that was being sent from Los Angeles.

It's an old Russian camera from the sixties, he said. It's difficult to find parts. Now we have to wait for them to come back. It's excruciating but we must be Zen about it.

I was so nervous. I felt like a moron. I stood there staring at them. I felt conspicuous in my long dress. I could feel the bobby pins from my *doak* stabbing me in the head. I could smell the cow shit on my shoes. I felt like Jonah after he'd been spit out of the whale onto dry land en route to wicked Nineveh. I didn't know what to say. There were no women in the house.

Where's Marijke the German star? I finally blurted out.

Diego whispered in my ear. She's in her room, crying. Let's go speak to her now. We walked down the long hallway to the back of the house. There were six or seven bedrooms that we passed to get to the very end. Diego pointed at each bedroom and told me which of the crew it belonged to. Somebody has painted an upside-down cross on mine, said Diego. Irma, did you know that Saint Peter asked specifically to be crucified upside down?

Nope, I said. I looked at Diego and smiled. It was a long hallway that led from Biblical times to the present and back again.

Out of humility, said Diego. To differentiate himself from Jesus Christ. The blood would have pooled in his head. I nodded. But I think, said Diego, that my crew meant it to be the sign of the Antichrist. They're funny guys.

Marijke had been given my aunt and uncle's former bedroom, the biggest one. Even the furniture was the same, and the bedding. My cousins had left in a hurry, apparently, and according to my dad it was because Wilf, the older boy, was a narco and about to be eviscerated by some rival narcos. My dad thought everyone who left Campo 6.5 was automatically a narco because why else would they be running away if they weren't narcos. If my dad's assessment was accurate this place was teeming with narcos, and not just garden-variety narcos but narcosatanics in search of sensations (like Jorge, allegedly), bored with drinking blood from skulls and poised to bolt for bigger thrills while the rest of us were in it for the long haul, working hard and honestly for very little money, the way God meant for us to be. But I didn't believe it. I think my uncle got a job selling cars in Canada and Wilf wanted to study the violin and my aunt thought it would be cool to get a perm. But who knows. Maybe they're a family of drug lords now, throwing bodies out of helicopters and bowling with the heads of double-crossers. That would be my father's theory.

Marijke was beautiful, strangely beautiful, like Diego had said. Everything about her seemed elongated, firm and far-reaching, like a tower crane or a tall, flightless bird. I imagined cowering under her wing in the rain. She was a Mennonite but she dressed differently than me. She dressed the way I had dressed in Canada, sort of. She had on skinny black jeans, like Miguel's, and a green T-shirt. She wasn't crying anymore. She was sitting cross-legged on her bed, on my aunt and uncle's bed, and smoking a slim Vantage cigarette. Diego greeted her in Spanish and kissed her cheek and she murmured something and smiled at me and asked me, in German, if I was the translator. I told her yes and we shook hands and then Diego said he'd leave us alone to talk.

What did he say? she asked me.

He just said hello, how are you, I said.

He's very polite, isn't he? she said.

Yes, I said. She looked around the room and then she walked over to the window and stared out at the yard. She was quiet, looking, and then she turned around and smiled at me again.

How old are you? she said.

Nineteen, I said. How old are you?

How old do you think I am? she asked.

I don't know, I said. Thirty?

I'll be forty-one in three weeks, she said.

You don't look forty-one, I said.

That's because something very traumatic happened to me when I was fourteen and as a result of that trauma I was prevented from moving forward, she said.

Oh, I said. But you will be forty-one in three weeks?

Technically, she said. On some level I've been alive for forty-one years but on other levels I stopped progressing at fourteen.

What happened to you when you were fourteen? I asked. I sat down on the bed beside her and she handed me her pack of cigarettes.

I'll tell you another time, she said. I have a son who isn't much younger than you.

How old is he? I asked.

He's sixteen, she said. But spiritually he's much older. I'd say closer to eighty.

I hope that someday somebody asks me where I was when I smoked my first cigarette so that I can tell them that yeah, well, you know, I was in my aunt and uncle's bed with this fourteen-year-old German actress who had an eighty-year-old son. No big deal. Marijke talked about her son, about missing him. She told me that she was worried that maybe she had been too much of a friend to her son lately and not enough of a parent.

Friends are good, she said, but sometimes a kid needs someone just to say hey, don't inject that, or whatever.

Are you from Russia? I asked her.

Yes, she said. I was born there but the place where I was born doesn't exist now.

What do you mean? I asked her. I was having a hard time following this conversation. I knew more about the social significance of birdsong, I realized, than I did about human interaction.

We talked about Diego and the crew and we talked about the script which I hadn't seen but which she told me was full of little drawings that accompanied the text and that she thought she'd be expected to take off her clothes for one or two scenes.

Do you want me to tell Diego that you don't want to take off your clothes? I asked her.

No, no, she said. That doesn't bother me. It's his story.

What is the movie about? I asked her.

Agony. And swimming. I don't know. I can't quite figure it out from the pictures and it's written in Spanish.

She asked me if I wanted to see the script and I said yeah but then she couldn't find it in her room and didn't want to go out to the main room to see if she'd left it there because she'd be expected to socialize with a bunch of people she couldn't communicate with beyond tequila and *danke schön* or learn how to juggle devil sticks or whatever they were doing in there.

I should go, I said. I was worried that Aggie would come looking for me here.

Why? said Marijke. You're nineteen years old! Are your parents that strict?

No, no, I said. My husband.

What? said Marijke. You're married?

Yeah, I said.

Does your husband mind that you're working as my translator?

No, I said. Not really. Well, actually, he doesn't know about it. He's been away for a while.

Well then, how would he be worried? she said. Why should you go home? She put her finger gently on the bumpy ridge between my eyes. Where your source of energy begins, she said. She kneaded the bumpy ridge gently with her long finger. I tried to speak and she said don't speak now, notice the light. Do you notice the light?

I don't know, I said. I have to do the milking or the cows will explode.

Is your husband a good kisser? she asked.

What? I said. Jorge? I don't know. I have nothing to compare him to.

We were quiet then, smoking, thinking about Jorge. At least I was. I think he might have been a good kisser. I pledged to tell him that if I ever saw him again. The cigarette was making me feel dizzy and I was trying not to cough.

Have you heard of the four-part cure, Irma? she asked.

No, I said. Cure for what? I stood up and looked around for a place to put my cigarette.

Here, said Marijke. She took it and put it in a glass of water next to her bed.

She said she had googled a new philosophy, a four-part cure, that would help her to live life on life's terms. She laid it out for me:

Don't fear God, she said.
Don't worry about death.
What is good is easy to get, and
What is terrible is easy to endure.

I'm quoting, she said. It's Epicurean. From a thousand years ago. People misinterpret Epicureanism these days. They misinterpret everything.

Plus, she said, I've learned that thoughts are atoms flying around in totally random patterns.

Oh, I said. They are?

That's all they are, she said. It'll help me in the desert. And I do believe in my soul. Anxiety's the killer.

Yeah, I said. That's true. Can I ask you a question?

Anything, she said. She squeezed my red, chapped hands and the room suddenly smelled like milk.

Why were you crying before? I asked.

Oh, that, she said. Okay, here's the thing. It's true that I have a new cure that I'm counting on to get me through life and it's true that I'm a little bit tough but the reality is that I'm a middle-aged woman in the middle of nowhere, a Mexican desert for God's sake, about to do something I have no experience doing and I'm feeling very, very alone and unsure and ridiculous and afraid.

Well, why did you agree to be in the movie? I asked her.

I'm not really sure, she said. Why did you agree to be my translator?

I'm not sure either, I said.

Well, I think I do know, actually, she said.

Yeah? I said. Why?

Because we were asked to, she said.

Oveja was stoned and following me from a distance. Elias, the cameraman, had told me on my way out that Oveja had eaten his stash of pot and that it had made him more philosophical. He'll think twice before he attacks, he said. Elias made me laugh. He didn't stop talking, like he didn't care that silence was supposedly golden, his currency was different. He had bought himself some clothes from the store in town, Wrangler jeans and a plaid shirt and work boots. Now I'm a Mennonite, he said. He told me that when he was a boy in Mexico City he had learned about Mennonites. He had seen some of them selling cheese on the streets and he had wanted to be one. Elias told me that he had even drawn a self-portrait of himself as a Mennonite in a bathtub. It's remarkable, he said, that now I'm making a film about them. He showed me a photograph of himself as a little boy on a beach in Acapulco. See that? he said. He told me that when he was a little boy he had an ass but that somehow, along the road to adulthood, he had lost his ass. Do you see? he said. He turned around so I could look at him. I thought he did have an ass but a small one. Look at Wilson, he said. He's got two asses and I have none. That's not fair.

Wilson ignored him completely. He was writing something down. Then he looked up and smiled at me and shrugged his shoulders. I'm Wilson, he said. That's fine, I said. Why did I say it was fine for him to be Wilson? I wanted to go back and tell him that I was Irma. But he knew that.

Diego asked me, before I left for home, if Marijke was okay and what we had talked about. She's fine, I said. Diego told me that the others had returned with the essential camera part and that tomorrow morning, early, we'd start shooting.

I was less afraid of Oveja now that he was a philosopher but I was nervous when he followed me home. I imagined his brown teeth sinking, pensively, into the back of my leg in search of something elusive. I thought about what Marijke had said. Oveja, I said, would you please stop following me? Asking didn't change anything with dogs.

Aggie was standing like a thief in the night at the dark end of my driveway. Her hair was tied back tightly, viciously. Her head shone like an egg.

What's wrong? I asked her.

What's that? she said, pointing at Oveja.

What's wrong? I asked her again.

Everybody hates you, she said. She kicked a bit of sand in my direction. Oveja sighed. What was the point. Stars fell.

That's not true, Aggie, I said. They don't care enough about me to hate me. You're the only one who does.

I don't hate you, said Aggie.

I know, I said. How do you like my new friend?

He's hideous, said Aggie. He's an asshole and he stinks like shit. I hope he gets run over by a baler.

We stood quietly and stared at the night. We were living in a dark, empty pocket. Not even the Hubble telescope could spot us on the earth's surface now.

Oh, c'mon, Aggie, I said. Stop crying. I wanted to tell her about the four-part cure. I wanted to convince her that everything good was easy to get and all that was terrible was easy to endure.

Hey Aggie, I said, you know what?

What? she said.

Oveja's stoned right now and thinks he's a philosopher. When it wears off he'll go back to attacking people. I don't think we have a lot of time. Then Aggie told me that her friend Aughte's dad, Alfredo, was going to play the husband in the movie. That Diego had promised him and his wife and kids a two-week all-inclusive resort package in Cancún when it was over and now everyone was mad at him too, and maybe after the movie they'd all move to a colony in Veracruz and she'd lose her best friend and Alfredo would find out that I was working for Diego too and tell our dad and that would be it, curtains.

And Mom's pregnant again, said Aggie. And doesn't want to get out of bed and doesn't smile anymore and I have to do everything now and Dad just yells and prays and I have chigoe bites all over my legs. So, why did you have to be such an idiot and go and marry a cholo?

He's not a narco, Aggie, I said. Let me see.

She lifted her dress a bit. There were ugly red sores all over her ankles and shins where the fleas had burrowed beneath her skin.

Let me sleep at your place tonight, Irma, please?

That night I had a dream about my mother and the next morning I saw her for the first time in months. I was up early, ready to start my new job, and I was standing in my yard waiting for the sun also to rise and warm me up. In my dream I was thinking about my dad yelling and praying and wondering if he got them mixed up sometimes and forgot who he was talking to. In my dream I looked at the road and there was my mother walking slowly, proud and majestic, or maybe just exhausted, like one of those giraffes you see briefly in shimmering sunlight on the savannah. She didn't look real and for a second I thought my mind had conjured up the thing it craved, the way a pregnant woman cries so she can taste the salt her body needs. Which is actually a lie my mother told us to explain away all her tears. But I was thinking about that stuff while I was running and then I was hugging her and I knew she was real because she was holding me so close to her it hurt and I was coughing trying to catch my breath and I could smell fresh bread and soap. I touched her stomach. She was farther along than I had thought.

Another one? I said.

Is Aggie with you? she said.

She's still asleep.

Send her home now, Irma, quickly.

I wanted to tell her about my dream but she had already begun to walk away and I stood there, like always, like forever it seemed, in the middle of the road waiting for something or someone to revive me, God or a parent or my husband or any of those things or people or ideas or words that by their definition promised love.

Diego suggested I keep a diary of "the shoot" after I mentioned a few things that Marijke had wondered about. For instance, why her character would be serene all the time. Was she in a depressive fog or not quite human or just plain stupid? He told me that he found it easier to understand certain ideas when he wrote them down or captured them on film and that I could try to do the same thing by keeping a diary of the shoot rather than by worrying about *his* ideas. Or something like that. He gave me a black notebook and a pen with a small light bulb on the tip.

Does this pen light up? I asked him.

Yes, there's a switch, he said. It doubles as a flashlight.

Thank you, I said.

The first thing I wrote down in my new notebook was:

YOU MUST BE PREPARED TO DIE!

That's what Diego told us this morning before we headed off to our first location. This is commando filmmaking, he said. The little red dot in the white of his left eye shone brighter than usual, like fresh blood on snow.

This is guerrilla filmmaking, he said. When it's time to work, it's time to work. If you're not prepared to risk your life, then leave now.

Irma, he said. Are you afraid?

Of dying? I said. I laughed out loud.

What is he saying? asked Marijke.

He wants us all to have fun, relax and be brave, I said.

I ran my fingernail over the leathery cover of the notebook and tried to carve my name into it. Then I thought to use the pen. I wrote my name on the inside cover and then crossed it out. I was afraid that my father would find it. I traced my left hand on a blank page and then filled it in with lifelines that somewhat resembled my own.

Diego has put Marijke into a dress like mine and tied her hair back with a kerchief and scrubbed off all her makeup. I explained to her that the first scene we'd be shooting was the family in their farmyard checking out a new tractor. We'd have to drive about an hour to the farmhouse where the scene would be shot. She stood in the yard like a smoking tree while the rest of us carried the equipment to the trucks.

Then Alfredo showed up with his wife and kids from Campo 3 a mile away, and they were not happy. I waved to them because I've known them all my life and Peter, the little boy who doesn't know any better, waved back. His older sister, Aggie's friend from school, pulled his hand down. They stayed in the truck and stared away at something. Alfredo ignored me and went over to Diego and told him that he had to quit.

What do you mean, quit? said Diego. What are you talking about? We haven't even started!

Alfredo told Diego that he was getting too much pressure from his wife and his parents. They didn't want him to act in a movie and it was taking him away from his work digging wells and his wife was jealous of his movie relationship with another woman.

Como lo arreglamos? said Diego. He wanted to know how they could work things out. Alfredo shrugged.

Diego smiled at me and then took Alfredo's arm and led him away behind the barn to talk about it and everybody standing around heard them yelling at each other in Spanish. Oveja went running around to the back of the barn to see what was going on and I heard Alfredo say he'd rip Oveja's jaw out and crush it under his truck tires if he came any closer. Then Diego yelled at Wilson to come and get Oveja and tie him to the pump.

What's the problem? Marijke asked me.

Nothing, I said. Diego is preparing Alfredo for his role.

At first Diego pleaded with Alfredo and then he was shouting, saying he had thought they had an understanding, and then he changed his strategy and appealed to Alfredo's ego (There is nobody, NOBODY, but you who can give this part the depth and humanity that it demands) and then he shifted his position again and offered him some more money and shortly after that they stopped yelling at each other and emerged from behind the barn and Alfredo went over to his wife and kids and talked to them and they drove off without waving and without Alfredo.

I don't want him to yell at me, said Marijke, if that's what it takes to prepare me. I can't handle that.

He won't, I said, your role is different.

We all piled into the trucks and drove off to shoot the first scene. Elias was driving the truck that Marijke and I were in. In Rubio, the closest village to our campo, he smashed it into a fence trying to back up and Diego, following behind, radioed him to let me drive because I knew the roads around there. We had to wait for a while so that Diego could negotiate something with the owner of the fence. Alfredo came over to where Marijke and I were standing and asked me if my father and my husband knew I was working for Diego.

When Diego came back he suggested that Alfredo change trucks and sit next to Marijke so they could get to know each other because they did speak the same language, but Marijke said that in fact their dialects were entirely different, she was a Russian Mennonite living in Germany and he was a Canadian Mennonite living in Mexico, and Alfredo was drunk and reeked of booze and was completely unintelligible and so . . . no.

She just wants some time to herself to organize her thoughts, I told Diego.

What thoughts? he said. Is she unhappy again?

I drove for a long time past various campos, clusters of barns and houses here and there, and down dirt roads and through cornfields and little streams and mud and desert. Elias and Sebastian, the sound guy, were sleeping in the back seat and Wilson sat in between them writing in his notebook.

What's he writing? Marijke asked me.

What are you writing? I asked Wilson, in Spanish, and he said stories, small stories. He said he'd like to read them at a festival in Guadalajara but he can't now because he's been commandeered to work for Diego and he needs the job.

Marijke, I said, does your husband mind that you're here in Mexico working on a movie?

No, she said, not at all. I don't think he does. Do I mind if he goes to work? Do I mind if he shits and breathes?

I thought, that's what I should have told Alfredo when he asked me about Jorge.

Elias woke up and lit a cigarette. I forgot my light meter, he said. I'm a dead man. Wilson looked up briefly from his writing.

We drove through clouds of dust in silence. We passed a few Tarahumara Indians on the road, a mother and her daughters clad in beautiful colours. They didn't seem to be walking anywhere. They were just there, standing brightly. I turned around to look a few times to see if they would move. I did it quickly, trying to catch them moving, but they had my number.

Marijke and I sat in an empty shed on upside-down feed buckets talking about the script and sex and the nervous system. She asked me if Jorge had wanted to have a baby with me.

I'm not sure, I said.

You didn't talk about it?

I don't think so, I said.

Would he make a good father, do you think? she said.

Well, I said, I'm not sure. What do you mean?

I mean would he be helpful with the baby and love it more than himself.

I was quiet, thinking of fathers, of my own and of Jorge's, who had watched his small shoes bubble over and then disappeared.

Well, what do you think? said Marijke. Are you crying?

Diego had asked me to do Marijke's hair like mine. I started combing it and a few chunks of it, long strands, fell onto the dirt floor. Those are my extensions, she told me. She told me they had been welded to her head with a heat gun and glue. She told me that mostly her hair would have to be braided and stuffed under her doak when she was acting but she thought there was one scene where it was required to tumble out of her kerchief and that's when she'd need the extensions.

I had that dreamy feeling of falling, for a split second, and then losing my footing again. To regain it, I tried quickly to remember the meaning of the word *samizdat*. And then I heard screams. A kid came running into the shed and grabbed my hand and dragged me outside into the yard where a bunch of other little kids were standing around a four-foot tiger snake. I grabbed a rake from the shed and neatly (not to brag, but you know) sliced the thing in two and the kids stared for a while, a couple of the boys kicked at it, and then went back to their game. Marijke came outside and asked me what was going on. Well, this thing is dead now, I said.

We stood with our hands on our hips and looked at it. Marijke's hair was half done and billowing out from one side of her head like the flag of some beautiful and indefinable region. She moved her fingers gently over the tight braids on the other side. Good job, she said.

Check this out, I said. I picked up a piece of the snake and peeled off its skin. I crushed the hard shell in my hand and showed Marijke the powder. You can sprinkle this over your food like salt, I said.

She licked her finger and dabbed at the crushed bits in my hand.

Hmmm, she said. Are you sure?

Diego called to say he needed Marijke then, to just shove the rest of her hair under the kerchief and come right now because the light was right and the Mennonites who owned the house were getting restless. The crew had set everything up and the Mennonite kids playing the Mennonite kids were in their places and their parents, Alfredo and Marijke, were supposed to talk about stuff while checking out the new tractor with the family. One of the kids didn't want to be there and Miguel was trying to cajole him in Spanish, which the kid didn't understand yet, and then to bribe him with chocolate. Eventually Miguel just said okay, go play, and he went out and plucked a different, more pliable blond-haired, blue-eyed kid from the crowd that had gathered around and set him down next to the tractor for the scene.

Diego asked Alfredo to remove his beer can from the hood of the tractor so it wouldn't be seen in the shot and then he took me aside and said that this was the scene of the family together, pivotal and establishing, and must be perfect. Alfredo will tell Marijke that he has to go to town on some kind of business and Marijke will indicate through her body language that she does not believe him but that she will accept what he is saying for the sake of peace in the home. Alfredo will take a few steps then come back and put his hand on her shoulder and tell her that he loves her. Marijke will tell him that she loves him too. Okay? he said. It's simple, right?

I nodded. Yeah, I said. Should I tell her now?

Yes, Irma, please, said Diego. We're ready. And can you also tell her to please not look into the camera.

I went over to Marijke and told her what Diego had said about not looking into the camera.

And when Alfredo tells you that he loves you, I said, you smile a little sadly and put your hand softly on his hand and tell him quietly that you're tired of his bullshit. In fact, no, not tired, but very close to being *defeated* by his bullshit.

That's what I tell him? she said.

Um, yes, I said. Quietly and sadly.

Okay, she said.

And remember the camera, I said. Not to look at it.

On the way home Elias and Sebastian smoked Faros and shared headphones.

Irma, said Elias. Do you know Neil Young?

Yeah, I said.

You do? said Elias.

No, I said.

He's from Canada! said Elias. He handed me his headphones and I put them in my ears and listened. I heard Neil Young singing about a sky about to rain.

What does that last part mean? said Elias.

I don't know, I said. Then I thought about it. I don't know, I said again.

It comes out of fucking nowhere but it fits perfectly, said Elias. I don't know what it means either but it's fucking brilliant. He took the headphones back and listened to another song. When it was finished he took them off and told us that the song was about this guy, he loses his way, his map, he loses his telescope, he loses his coastline! It's so great, he loses everything, he loses his words! So he keeps singing but just this la la la la la la la la and it gets more and more joyful and builds into this incredible crescendo, it's so happy, because he's finally free and he's lost but he's free!

Marijke slept with her rubber boots up on the dash and Wilson wrote in his notebook.

Hey Wilson, said Sebastian. What are you writing about?

Nothing, said Wilson. He closed his notebook and put it on the seat beside him.

C'mon, you're writing something, said Sebastian. What is it? A love letter? Is it about us?

No, said Wilson. Fuck off.

C'mon, said Sebastian. What are you writing? Tell us.

I'm writing about how dreams are like art and how both are sort of a conjuring up of the things that we need to survive.

That's why I always dream about sex, said Elias.

Even if it's an unconscious or subconscious act, said Wilson. Art, of course, is a more wilful act than a dream, but it comes from the same desire to live.

I once had a dream that I was fucking the world, said Elias. Like, I don't know how old I was but I was in Montevideo in a house somewhere and I was bored so I wandered around and then I got this idea so I went to the back door and I opened it and stepped outside and took my dick out and started banging the night. Like, I was just banging away at the night. But the night was dark, obviously, so there was no stopping it. I mean I couldn't see where the night ended, because of the horizons or whatever, so it was like the night was the whole world and I was fucking it.

You weren't fucking the world, said Sebastian. You were jerking off in the dark like every other night.

No, man, said Elias. It seemed like that but it was different in my dream.

I'm talking about dreams of guilt and dreams of redemption, said Wilson.

We don't know it but we direct our own dreams, said Sebastian. A restructuring or an un-structuring of ideas and experiences that allow for our own salvation.

Give that to me, said Wilson. You're an asshole.

Our dreams are little stories or puzzles that we must solve to be free, Sebastian said. He was reading out loud from Wilson's notebook. My dream is me offering me a solution to the conundrum of my life. My dream is me offering me something that I need and my responsibility to myself is to try to understand what it means. Our dreams are a thin curtain between survival and extinction.

Sebastian, said Wilson. Can I have that, please?

I like it! said Sebastian. No, seriously, that's heavy shit that clarifies a thing or two for me.

Sebastian, said Wilson. Please?

Sebastian handed over Wilson's notebook and apologized for reading from it. Wilson waved it all off and smiled at me as if to say, would you help me blow up the universe?

Well, said Elias, my dream is me telling me to fuck the world. That's my art. What can I say.

Wilson stared out the window and Elias and Sebastian went back to listening to their music. I looked at Marijke. She was still sleeping. Then she opened one eye halfway and looked at me as though she was incorporating me into her dream and closed it again. I drove slowly, trying to relate everything to a dream, hoping to see my Tarahumara family again before the dream ended.

THREE

IT WAS LATE WHEN WE GOT BACK to the filmmakers' house. Wilson invited me in for coffee and I said no, I couldn't. Then I changed my mind and said yeah, okay. He told me he wanted to show me something. Marijke had gone to her room and closed the door—we could hear her laughing or crying—and Diego was busy talking on the radio. Wilson asked me if I would come into his bedroom. I stood still and quietly panicked and then he said that it was okay, he didn't mean it in that kind of way, he just wanted a little privacy from the others. So I followed him into his room and he closed the door and I went and stood by the window and he sat on his bed.

I'd like to read you something if you don't mind, Irma, he said. He opened his notebook and read a story, half in Spanish, half in English, about an angry circus clown who was going through a divorce.

All the people in my stories are awful, he said. I agreed with him.

Why don't you write about people who aren't such assholes? I asked him.

Because, he said, that would be too painful.

I looked around the room. I remembered playing with my cousins. I remembered trying to climb out the window of this room and breaking the window frame. I got up and went over to the window and it was still cracked and crooked.

I used to play here all the time, I said.

Really? said Wilson.

Yeah, my cousins lived here.

One family? said Wilson. There are so many bedrooms in this house.

Lots of kids, I said. A soccer team.

Or a film crew, said Wilson.

They didn't make movies, I said.

I know, said Wilson, I was just kidding. They probably didn't play soccer either.

Of course they played soccer, I said. That's mostly what we did all the time.

Oh, said Wilson. Are you any good?

Not really, I said.

Do you want to kick a ball around sometime? said Wilson.

Well . . . I don't know, I said. I'm a married woman now.

So? said Wilson.

I could see Elias and Sebastian standing on the road talking to each other and passing a cigarette back and forth. Elias was waving his arms around and Sebastian was perfectly still. Corn was behind them. Endless corn. Then Elias crouched down to the ground and picked up some stones and threw them at the corn and there was a dark explosion of crows.

Why is it so painful to write about people who aren't assholes? I asked Wilson.

Because I would start to love them, he said.

I was still looking through the broken window. I didn't know what to say. I heard Wilson sigh. Can I show you something now? he asked. I went over to the bed and stood beside him and he lifted up his shirt. There were scars all over his chest and stomach, some of them looping around to his back.

What happened? I asked him.

I'm dying, he said. I sat down beside him on the bed.

From what? I said.

My veins won't stay open, he said. They sometimes just collapse. The doctors have cut me open so many times to work on a vein but after a few months another vein quits and they have to go back in. Then they gave me this super-industrial-strength medicine that I had to squirt into my body through a tap in my stomach. They drilled a hole right here above my belly button and stuck a little faucet in there that was attached to a long cord and a pump which I could hold in my hand and every hour or so I'd have to squirt another drop into my body and it would go through the long cord and then through that little tap into my gut. It was basically like TNT blasting through my veins trying to wake them up so the blood could move.

You don't have the tap anymore? I said.

No, said Wilson, because I kept getting infections from the incision and they had to replace it every three weeks and that was excruciating. So now it's just a matter of waiting. But I try not to think about it.

Are you afraid? I asked him.

He told me he was scared shitless, actually, who wouldn't be? And then I told him about all the stupid things I'd done in that room when I was a kid and a little bit about my old life in Canada, how we couldn't recognize even our own mothers in the winter because we were so bundled up trying to stay warm, which he thought was funny. And I told him about the hockey rink that my father built for us little kids in our backyard by first of all clearing away tons and tons of snow and then using that snow to build towering walls around the rink and then by packing down the surface until it was as smooth as glass even though it was only rock-hard snow and how once I woke up in the middle of the night and the yard light was still on which made me wonder what was going on so I looked out the window at the glistening hockey rink in our backyard and

I saw my father on his hands and knees in the middle of it next to a perfect red circle and he was all hunched over and concentrating, painting lines, red ones and blue ones, on the hard snow to make the hockey rink official and the lines were so even and perfect and bright against the white snow. I watched him paint for a long time and finally he stood up and put his hands on his hips like this and stared at his circle and his lines and he had this huge grin on his face.

Did he see you in the window? said Wilson.

No, I don't think so, I said.

Was it supposed to be a surprise for you guys? said Wilson.

Yeah, I said. The next morning we went downstairs and we went outside and he was there with new hockey sticks for all of us too. We had to make up names for our teams and sing the national anthem.

Beautiful, said Wilson. Did you play on it?

Yeah, we played forever, I said. Not with skates or anything, just in our boots. Sometimes, my older sister, Katie, would referee for a while before she got bored and went off with her friends. Every night until way past everyone else had gone to bed. So it was me and my mom against my dad and Aggie. She was little and he made sure she got a shot every once in a while and me and my mom would fake trying really hard not to let it in.

But somehow it got in, said Wilson.

Yeah, I said. And then she and my dad would do their victory dance.

Do you think it's still there? said Wilson.

Well, I said. You know what happens to snow, sometimes, right?

Two things happened when I got back to my house. Somebody was sitting at the kitchen table in the dark. I thought it was Jorge and I was about to jump on top of him but then I realized it was my father.

That was the first thing. And the second thing is that he spoke to me. But not until after a long period of spooky silence. Just sitting there and looking at me or looking around the house.

So what's up? I asked him finally. Is mom okay?

You're involved with the filmmakers? he said. I didn't say anything.

And Aggie is also spending time with you? he said.

She's my sister, I said.

She's my daughter, he said. I'm thinking of selling your house.

Well, where will I live? I asked him.

He suggested I talk to God about that and reminded me that the house belonged to him and that he had only allowed Jorge and me to live in it because we were also taking care of his cows but now I was getting Aggie to do the work and running around with artists, and my husband should be the one to take care of me and now I was humiliating everyone, my mother, my father, my relatives, the entire campo, the church and God.

What about the cows? I said. You forgot to mention.

You're not funny, Irma, he said.

Well, you're not either, I said. I guess the apple doesn't fall too far from the tree.

What apple? he said.

Me, I said. I'm the apple and you're the—

You're a lunatic, he said.

Jorge hasn't left me, I said. My father looked around the house pretending to search for Jorge like it was a joke. I stood up. I wasn't afraid of him for myself, only for Aggie, but I was going to leave.

Irma, said my father, what do you want from this life?

I sat down next to him and touched his arm for half a second. It was a surprise and he didn't flinch. He didn't expect an answer. It was a kind gesture for any man from around here to ask a question of his daughter. I felt like touching his arm again but I knew he'd be prepared this time and pull away.

You don't have light in here? he said.

Sometimes, I said. I can't get the generator to work. I had a flashlight but I lost it. He didn't say anything. For a second I was sure that he would promise to come back to fix the generator. I knew he wanted to. I waited for him to say the words. Then he got up and left. It felt like a scene in the movie. I imagined my father saying hey, how was that? Was I okay? And I'd say well, it wasn't bad, but let's do it one more time.

We were in an apple orchard with an old, slimy swimming pool in the middle. An ancient Mexican woman in a Nike T-shirt had opened up the wire gate for us and led us to the pool. I had wandered off into the trees to pee and while I was squatting in the dappled sunlight a huge horse appeared out of nowhere and tried to push me over with its nose. Fuck off, I said, and then apologized. I picked up a rotten apple that had fallen onto the ground and tossed it gently at the horse and it moved a foot or two away from me and snorted like it was planning to charge and then changed its mind and came back and stood next to me, over me really, while I finished peeing. If I could only interpret my dreams I would know what I wanted from this life and then I'd be able to explain that to my father. I felt sleepy, so tired. I thought about having a short nap while the horse watched over me. Horse, I said, what are you doing here? He let that question dangle between us and I left.

It was another shot of the family, this time swimming together but with undercurrents of tension. On the surface the shot was supposed to be serene and warm and show the hard-working family having a nice little break. Diego was having a heart-to-heart conversation with Alfredo about the necessity of him taking his clothes off in the abandoned change room.

Marijke doesn't have a problem taking off her clothes, said Diego.

She's European, said Alfredo.

It will be a long shot, Alfie, said Diego. You'll be this big. He held his fingers up an inch apart. And it's dark in there. It will be one brief second in the film.

Marijke was lying in the sun reading a book called *You Are Not a Stranger Here* and smoking and Miguel was running around with the Mennonite children, trying to keep them from getting bored while the others set up the shot. A crowd of people from the nearby campo, including the mothers and siblings of the kids acting in the movie, had found out where we were shooting and were standing around watching.

One of the mothers came up to me, her name was Tina, and she asked me how my mother was and I said I didn't know really but that she was going to have another baby and then Tina asked me if I knew that Aggie had quit school to help out at home.

When did that happen? I said.

I think today, she said.

I thought of my father making a long slit in the stomach of a hog and draining its blood and guts onto the ground in minutes. In seconds. In one second. Which was the length of time it took for news to spread around here.

I wasn't surprised at all and I wanted to talk to Tina some more about Aggie just to be able to form the shape of her name with my lips and my tongue, Aggie, but Diego called *my* name and I had to go.

Tina, I said, will you ask Abe to talk to my father about Aggie staying in school?

What would I say? said Tina.

I don't know, I said. But my father has always liked Abe and maybe he can say something.

Tina nodded and touched my shoulder. She told me she would pray for our family. She told me that Abe liked my father too, but didn't like how strict he was. She said that she and Abe were grateful to my father for not involving the police when their son shot one of our cows just for fun.

Thanks, I said. Can you please tell my mother hello and how are you.

Diego called me again and Tina and I said goodbye. He was still trying to convince Alfredo to get naked and Alfredo was sitting on a rock enjoying another vampiro and smoking and shaking his head and Diego told me to tell Marijke that when Alfredo told her what a good mother she was, in the scene, that she should tell him that he was a good father, too. And that when Alfredo commented on her soap-making abilities that she acknowledge him gratefully with something appropriate.

I began to walk over to where Marijke was and Diego began yelling at Alfredo that okay, fine, he'd take his clothes off too, for the shot, no sweat. And then he told the crew that they should take theirs off too so that Alfredo could see that he wasn't the only man in the world with a cock and balls and they said sure, no problem, and began to strip down to their underwear and Marijke was looking at them all calmly, smoking, and I started to panic and ran over to Diego and told him that they couldn't do that, that all the Mennonites watching would seriously freak out and the crew would be herded up and shot and left in a field to rot and their faces sewn into soccer balls.

All right, said Diego, we'll shoot that part another time when nobody is watching. He put his pants back on but by this time Elias, Sebastian and Wilson were all in the pool in their underwear trying to keep the camera from slipping off the inner tube that they had tied it to. Some of the women watching had taken their kids away and a few of them were standing with their arms folded laughing at the half-naked crew and whispering. I ran back to Marijke and sat down with her in the sun and she put her arms around my shoulders and asked me how things were going.

Life is a bitter gift, no? she said.

So, now, in this shot, I said, when Alfredo tells you that you're a good mother you smile softly, like this, and look at him and say thank you, but how would you know? And when Alfredo tells you that you make good soap or whatever his line is you nod and say yes, but you're sick of making soap and thinking of just buying it in the store from now on. And again, I said, try not to look directly at the camera. Marijke nodded and got up. Thanks, Irma, she said.

No sweat, I said.

We smiled and I told her she was beautiful. Radiant. I told her I thought her neck was as long if not longer than my forearm, like Nefertiti. She told me she felt like shit in the dress she was wearing and then looked at mine and apologized and said that it was weird that her dress was a costume and mine was just a dress even when they were virtually identical and then she apologized again, she put her hand on her throat as though that was the place where regrettable words sprang from, and I waved it all away, it didn't matter. I had befriended a horse wearing this dress. For some reason I thought it would be funny for me to tell Marijke that but she was already gliding away towards Diego and the others.

The next day everybody was sick, probably from the dirty water in the pool and nobody had anything to say. Through the kitchen window I could see Oveja napping under the truck. I pulled the notebook from the pocket of my dress and pressed it to my forehead. It felt cool on my warm skin.

> Diego has asked me if I'd be willing to clean the house and do the crew's laundry. Marijke and the crew are huddled around the TV watching something with no sound and looking green and exhausted. I don't know how to ask Diego if he'll pay me extra for cleaning. In addition to the word *samizdat* I'm now pondering the meaning of the word *despondent*. My English is fine. I lived in Canada for thirteen years and went to a normal school with normal kids. But there are words that drift around in my head like memories from the Jazz Age or something. I want to say them but they're not really mine to feel. Here comes Diego again. The end.

Okay, I said. I'll clean the house.

He said he'd still take the crew out to shoot some stuff but that Marijke could have the day off and stay in bed or do whatever she wanted to do.

Where's Wilson? I asked.

He went back to Caracas, said Diego.

Why? I said.

We had a fight, said Diego. I keep forgetting how sensitive he is. He erupts like shrapnel and then goes psycho still, like numb inside. His eyes go like this. I don't understand him. He wants me to write an introduction to his book of stories. But now we all have extra work. Irma, I have a question to ask you. Do you know that song "A Hard Rain's A-Gonna Fall"? Do you know this? *A-gonna*?

No, I said.

Diego went back into the living room to talk to the others and I wandered into Wilson's room and looked around. He wasn't there. So, that was true at least. I sat on Wilson's bed and felt the mattress sag a bit beneath me. He hadn't forgotten to take his notebook.

After the others had left, Marijke went into the yard and threw up next to the pump. She washed her face and then stuck her whole head under the water and then took off her T-shirt and lay on the grass on her back with her breasts exposed to the sun and the wind and God. I lay down in the grass on my side with my back to her.

Marijke, I said, what kind of a Mennonite are you? I said it quietly and in Spanish. In fact, I may not have said it at all.

Irma, she said, do you have any real idea of what this movie is about?

Well, it's about the meaning of life? I said. I mean not life, life, but some lives? That's all I can think of. Leave-taking.

What did you say? she said.

Leave-taking, I said. I wasn't sure how to use that word in a sentence. Our leave-taking from Canada was abrupt and permanent. Our poignant leave-taking left me breathless and . . . I wasn't sure.

You miss Wilson, she said. I didn't say anything. I couldn't see her. She put her hand on my back and I went stiff like a stillborn calf. I felt like I was being branded. I thought I'd start to cry.

No, I said, I miss Jorge.

When we first got married Jorge was at home all the time but then he went to his mom's place in Chihuahua city one weekend to visit and he met some guys who offered him real money. All he'd have to do was store their boxes of *hierba* in our grain shed because we lived in the middle of nowhere but only a few hours from the border and it was all perfect, and Jorge said sure, that sounded good, all he'd be doing was storing it, and he had held my hands and told me it would be a great opportunity for us, that it might help us to make enough money to leave the campo so he wouldn't have to work for nothing for my father anymore and he'd take care of me and we'd have babies and move away from here and get that boat we'd been talking about. And then he started bringing stuff back to our place.

I think Diego might want to sleep with me, she said.

What? I said. Why do you think that? You don't even know what he's saying.

I don't have to know what he's saying, she said.

Well, I said. I wouldn't if I were you.

Why not? she said. What if I'm feeling lost and lonely?

Are you? I said.

Of course I am, Irma! she said. Look around. Can I talk to anybody but you? Do I have my husband and son here with me? Do I have friends? Do I know what I'm doing? Do I understand this story? Do I have anything to do but lie around and try to remember not to look directly at the thing that's always looking at me?

No, I said. I guess not.

I'm trying not to let my anger bubble to the surface and infect my mood, she said. Have you ever stomped down on a ceramic tile on your kitchen floor? It keeps popping up. I'm not going to sleep with him, don't worry.

I'm not worried, I said.

My anger, I said to myself. I liked the sound of that. I needed something of my own, something I could keep. My anger. I'd embroider these words into my underwear. I felt like Frankenstein. I punched myself in the forehead. My mother thought I was retarded when I was a baby because I'd bite myself and pull my own hair. Well, whose hair was I supposed to pull? I'd ask her.

Marijke lit a cigarette and started humming.

Well, the tile just needs to be glued down, I said.

Hey, she said, do you mind asking Diego if it's possible to get more leafy vegetables around here? I was looking at the whites of my eyes this morning and I think I'm developing anemia.

I turned around and looked deeply into the whites of her eyes and tried to detect a problem.

Then she told me she'd like to meet my family and I told her why that was pretty much impossible and then just at that moment as though we'd conjured her up like a dream Aggie was standing next to us with a suitcase and there we were, three Mennonite girls in an empty field, one bare-chested, one bewildered and one on the run.

Diego and the crew came roaring back into the yard in two trucks and Elias and Oveja ran over to us and Elias said we had to go shoot right then, immediately. Because the light, he said. And we had to bring Oveja with us for some reason

I couldn't quite understand. Either because we would need protection or because he, Oveja, needed protection.

What did you say? said Aggie.

Who is this? said Elias. He smiled and kissed Aggie on the cheek.

Aggie, I said. My sister. This is Elias. He's a cameraman. This is Marijke.

Did you come from the airport? said Elias. He pointed at her suitcase.

No. Just from over there, said Aggie. She pointed at her house.

Come with us, said Marijke. She put her T-shirt back on and grabbed Aggie's suitcase. It'll be fun.

No, I said, she has to go back.

No, I don't, said Aggie.

Yeah, you do, I said.

Well, I'm not, she said.

Agatha, I said.

Irma, she said.

We rode in the back of the truck this time while Diego drove and had a money talk with one of the film's producers, José. We could see their arms flying around in the cab while they talked. Elias told us that José had come from Mexico City with some concerns about the amount of money Diego was spending out here in Chihuahua. Diego was having to shell out dough like crazy to the various Mennonites he'd enlisted to help him realize his dream. Elias explained Diego's rationale with the campo dwellers. This is what he says, said Elias. I understand and respect your religion's stance on photography and artificial images but I also believe that by making this film we can help to preserve your culture and prevent it from disappearing. This presented a conundrum that stopped the Mennonites in their argumentative tracks. Diego then added that he was willing to pay them for letting him shoot on their land, or in their house, or wherever it was that he wanted to shoot, and that got the Mennos nodding again and shortly thereafter the deal was done.

That's what they're talking about, said Elias. Diego is trying to explain to José the reason why the Mennonites are being truculent. No offence.

I had stopped listening, really, because now Aggie and I had started to argue.

Marijke and the crew smoked and stared politely into the desert pretending not to notice me and Aggie hissing at each other in the wind. She kept her hand on the handle of her suitcase but she turned her head away from me when I tried to talk to her.

So, where do you think you're going to go? I said.

Don't worry about it, she said.

Well, obviously I'm going to worry about it, I said. Are you a total moron or what?

Let's enjoy the moment, Irma, she said. She was quoting Marijke. José and Diego were shouting and throwing cigarettes out the windows. A spark skittered off the metal and landed on Elias's arm and he swore in Spanish, *puta*, and extinguished it with his spit. Trucks packed full of Mexican or Mennonite families were passing us and they were all waving and smiling or very determinedly looking away, like

Aggie when I tried to tell her that she was risking her life by leaving home.

I know, she said. So what. I didn't know what to say then and wished that I smoked for real or that sparks would land on me.

Because the light, said Aggie.

What? I said.

Because the light, she said. What that guy said. She pointed at Elias who blew her a kiss. It's funny, she said.

Stop taking my things, I said. I pointed at her ratty suitcase.

I'm returning it to you, she said.

We're standing, lying, sitting in an empty field
waiting for the rain. This time Aggie is with us,
learning how to play Frisbee with Miguel and
Elias, and apparently enjoying the moment as
though it were her last. Oveja has now become
her best friend thanks to a dozen zwieback she
had in the suitcase. Alfredo has come here in his
own truck, by himself, but he's sulking and
Diego is worried about him leaving before the
rain comes. Alfredo says he is wasting his time
and losing money that he could be making from
his real job and that there's so much stress at
home because of this movie. Diego has taken
me aside and asked me, again, to ask Marijke if
she would spend more time with Alfredo. If
maybe now she would agree to drive with
Alfredo in his truck so that they can get to know

each other and so that Alfredo won't feel lonely
and ignored.

I took Marijke aside to tell her what Diego had told me. I handed her my bottle of water.

He would like you to spend more time alone with Alfredo, I said.

Why? said Marijke.

To strengthen your relationship.

What relationship?

Your movie relationship.

That's Diego's job, she said. She drank the water that was left in the bottle and gave it back to me.

Diego jogged over to us. He looked worried. He was wearing white, gauzy pants that billowed out like sails when he ran. From a distance his head was a crow's nest. He asked me if I had told Marijke what he had said about spending time with Alfredo.

Yes, I said, but she has reservations.

Please tell her that it's important for the energy of the film, said Diego. Please tell her that when I see a beautiful fish I immediately have feelings for it. I wait until the last possible moment to cook it. And it's that connection that makes the meal delicious.

Marijke, I said, Diego wants you to know that he sometimes has feelings for beautiful fish before he eats them and that makes them taste better.

Is he stoned? said Marijke.

Hang on, I said. I spoke to Diego in Spanish. Yeah, I said, she understands. But she doesn't want to drive with him because he's always drunk and she's not prepared to die.

Irma, said Diego, when I said we must all be prepared to die for this film, I didn't mean in a car crash because of drunk driving. If that's what you're implying. Tell her I'll talk to Alfredo about his drinking.

Well, I said. And she's worried about having anemia. She needs more leafy vegetables.

We continued to wait in the field for rain. José and Diego played a game that involved slapping each other hard in the face. José seemed to be winning and Diego refused to give up. Why are they doing that? Aggie asked me.

Elias heated up some sausages on a filthy grill over an open fire. I taught Marijke how to make a type of kissing sound that would keep the rattlesnakes away when she went into the trees to pee. José and Diego ended their strange game with an embrace. The sun scorched us. Diego tried to get Marijke to rehearse a kiss with Alfredo and eventually became so angry with Alfredo's clunky attempts that he grabbed Marijke and did it himself. Is that so difficult? he asked Alfredo.

Afterwards Marijke came up to me and asked me if I knew what she meant about Diego having the hots for her and I said yes. We sat on the ground and flipped through the pages of the script. It was clear that Diego had started to make things up along the way.

Aggie came to sit with us and had a look at the script too, and I asked her what she thought. I don't understand all the Spanish, it's a bit majestic, I guess, she said. I liked the offhanded way she neutered words that were meant to be powerful. Then all the men started yelling at each other about the new Mexican president and the fraudulent election. The Zócalo in Mexico City was filled with thousands and thousands of protesters. They've been there for a week already, said Diego, and they refuse to budge. He said he thought it made more sense to wait for rain in the desert than for justice in Mexico City.

The clouds were moving around, bulging and darkening here and there but nothing else. It was getting late and I had to get Aggie home before my dad got back from the field or from town or wherever he was. She and I were still arguing. I told her that she was risking a lot by being out here with the film crew and that she was being foolish. I told her how much her brazenness bugged me because she didn't have a clue what she was doing.

Well, why are you here then, Irma? she said. You're a hypocrite.

I'm here because it's a job and I have no money and no family. Nothing! I said. I have nothing to lose. You should go home and stay away from me.

I was starting to sound like Jorge.

You can't tell me what to do, she said.

You're an idiot, I said. You have no idea.

Most of the crew had fallen asleep on a tarp, surrounded by equipment and empty water bottles, and Diego and José were talking quietly in the truck. I knocked on the window.

I need to get Aggie home, I said.

Diego got out of the truck and stood there squinting

up at the sky. We'll give up on today, he said. I thought it was the rainy season now.

It's supposed to be, I said.

Do you think God is punishing us? said Diego.

Why, what did you do? I said. He told me he was just joking.

Will you be able to make a meal for the crew when we get back? he said. A woman from the village was supposed to come but she took my money and never came. Her brother told me she went to America. Or she is dead. I'm not sure.

I'm not sure I have time, I said. Aggie has to get back and I'm worried—

Now you're worried, said Diego. First Marijke, now you. You girls are professional worriers, I'll say this.

I'm not going back, Irm, so don't worry your pretty little head over me, said Aggie.

You don't know that expression, I said.

You don't know everything, said Aggie.

We'll stop and buy some food and it'll be green and good for your anemia, said Diego.

Not mine, Marijke's, I said.

Okay, said Diego. I could make it myself but José and I have paperwork to fill out and the guys are still feeling a little sick. Plus, I promised in their contracts there would be meals and I'm worried about a mutiny. Please, Irma, I really need your help.

I didn't say anything. I waited to feel that old familiar pain in my chest, my cue to continue.

I'll do it, said Aggie.

No, you won't, I said. She can't.

Why not? said Diego. It makes no difference, you or her.

I want to do it, said Aggie.

No, I'll do it, I said. It's fine. No sweat.

Aggie started to say something to me in German, but Diego cut her off in English. You and Aggie can sit in the cab with José and me, said Diego. Marijke will drive with Alfredo.

What? I said. I told you, remember, that Marijke doesn't want to drive with Alfredo. She's worried that—

It's all right, said Diego. I talked to Alfredo. I ran four times around the pasture with him and afterwards he was healthy.

José opened the passenger door for Aggie and me and we got in. Oveja jumped up and down throwing himself against the window, crying and howling. Aggie said we had to let him in and Diego said no, not possible, he had to ride in the other truck and Aggie said fine, let her out then, but the other truck had already taken off so Diego had to let Oveja ride with Aggie. The truck got stuck in the muddy field and we had to push ourselves out and José helped but fell and was covered completely in mud and very angry because he hadn't brought extra clothes from Mexico City. We had to stop all over the place to buy supplies, food and water and beer and gas and some new pants for José.

Aggie and Oveja and I sat on a box outside a store in Rubio and looked around. Aggie couldn't remember the last time she'd been to town. She was making some jokes and goofing around but I was trying to ignore her. Did you know that there's this country that nobody really knows about that's kept in an office building in Paris? she said.

A girl wandered over to us and asked if she could sit down too, and we all moved over a bit and waited. She didn't look much older than Aggie. She was drinking some juice out of a plastic bag. She told us her name was Lindsay Beth and that she was from Indianapolis. We told her we were Irma and Aggie from nearby and that the dog was Oveja.

Why are you dressed like that? she said. We shrugged and looked around some more. That a pit bull? she asked. We nodded.

Are you here all by yourself? said Aggie.

Yeah, she said. They had to keep me in a cage.

Who kept you in a cage? said Aggie.

Rehab, she said. She told us they had thrown a box of soap in her cage and she was supposed to use it to carve her urges into shapes and she'd carved a giant key.

I would kill for OxyContin, she said.

Then how are you allowed to travel all by yourself? I asked her.

It's about establishing trust, she said.

What is OxyContin? said Aggie.

This is the last time my parents are going to bail me out, said Lindsay Beth. I'm not actually by myself.

She was wearing pyjama bottoms that said *dark side of the moon* all over them. A little boy who had been playing around in the dirt came over and practised his reading on her legs. He poked at her pyjamas. His small finger traced the words. Dark. Side. Of. The. Moon, he said. Dark side of the moon. Dark side of the moon. Dark side of the . . . He pulled the fabric a bit where it had crinkled . . . moon.

This is my brother's kid, she said. We waved at him.

Where's your brother? I asked her.

Inside, she said. We're on our way to the last ditch hotel. They're supposed to make excellent smoothies there, that's all I know, and that's all my stomach can absorb. My brother will drop me off and only pick me up again if I'm clean at the end of it. Otherwise I'll just be released into the atmosphere like a toxic gas. I'll just wander around the desert like Neal Cassady or whatever and eventually lie down for a nap on railway tracks.

She told the kid to go and find his dad. She told us that her brain had disintegrated to the point where her eyeballs had minds of their own and that even when she knew she was staring straight ahead her eyeballs would do their own thing and look elsewhere, off to the side or up towards the sky. She told us that even her one-thousand-dollar-a-day rehab facility in Malibu with equine therapy had failed to take. They think my brother will help me but he won't. He's fed up. She pointed at the store. I have to want to stay alive or not. I told her it looked like she wanted to.

Do you? said Aggie. She had stood up and was facing Lindsay Beth with her hands on her hips.

Well, she said, I want my hair to stop falling out. She pulled out a chunk of her hair and showed it to us. She held it tenderly in her hand like a wounded bird. Aggie stared at it for a long time and seemed distressed when the girl finally threw it into the wind and it flew off towards El Paso. We talked for a while about things and played a little hide-and-seek game with the boy and waited and waited.

FOUR

BY THE TIME WE GOT HOME a little apocalypse was brewing. I saw smoke coming from the field behind my house and told Aggie to stay put and then ran over to investigate. I saw the car. I saw the fire. I saw Jorge.

You're home! I said. I ran up to kiss him and hug him. I wanted to touch him. I wanted to feel the hard slope of his back. I wanted to put my head under his shirt and pin him to the ground and listen to his heart beating but he was busy throwing stuff into the fire.

Where were you? he asked.

Where were *you*? I said.

Help me put this shit away, he said. We carried his boxes into the back shed and he hoisted them up into the rafters. After that he relaxed a bit and smiled and even made a few jokes and was almost like his old self and we went into the house and I made him something to eat and he gave me a new pair of sunglasses which I put on and then he gave me a new pair of jeans which I also put on under my dress.

We fooled around for a while, throwing grapes into each other's mouths and then bouncing them off the wall and seeing if we could still catch them in our mouths.

How's your mom? I asked him.

Good, he said. Says hi.

Jorge said he wanted to teach me some dance move he'd learned in Chihuahua city. You stand like this, he said. He turned me around so he was behind me.

How'd you learn this dance? I said.

Then slowly grind down to the floor by moving your hips like this, he said. He demonstrated.

But where'd you learn to dance like this? I said.

Like a rotor, he said, and while you're doing that, I'll stand behind you with my hands on your hips like this and I'll grind down too. Okay, go. Slowly.

I tried to remember the instructions. I knew the objective was to get down to the floor in a squatting position.

No, he said, you're dropping way too fast, like you're dodging a punch or something. You have to make small, slow circles with your hips, like gradually, until you're down. I tried again.

Irma, he said, it's not that hard. What's your problem? Look. He showed me what to do.

See? he said. Stop laughing. Try again.

I stood up and shook my head. I can't, I said. I'm sorry, but—

Take your dress off, he said. Okay?

I don't have a top on under, I said.

Yeah, I know, he said. That's okay, it's nice. It'll be nice. I took my dress off and stood there topless in my new stiff jeans and sunglasses.

Yeah, he said, you look good. That's nice. Okay, let's try it again. He stood behind me and put his hands on my hips and we began to grind. He whispered in my ear. Slowly, Irma, he said. Even slower. He slid his hands up to my breasts and played with my nipples. In circles, Irma, he said. Move your hips in circles. Yeah. Do you feel me? I could hear him breathing. Okay, and down now, Irma, but slowly, really— Fuck! Irma. What the hell is your rush? Look, I'm up here still and you're down there crouching like you're taking a dump.

I don't know, I said. I don't get the move. I'm sorry. It feels weird.

Jorge sat down at the table and rubbed his eyes and sighed.

Irma, he said, I'm trying to improve our lives.

I know, I said. I'm sorry. Can we try it again?

I'm so tired, he said. He took my hand and kissed it.

I'm sorry, I said again.

I'm sorry too, he said.

I miss you, I said.

Irma, I'm so tired now, he said. But I can't sleep anymore.

Why don't you try sleeping now? I said. I could lie down with you until you fall asleep.

I'm not a little kid, he said. He put his head down on the table and I rubbed his back and kissed his hair.

Are you tired of being a man? I asked him.

Why would you say that? he said. That's so messed up. Are you tired of being a girl?

Yeah, sometimes, I said.

Well, why would you even think that? said Jorge. Irma, you have to stop talking that shit. Do you want to become a man?

No, I said. It's not that. I'm just asking if—

Fuck it, he said. Never mind.

I told you I was sorry, Jorge, I said. I can't do that dance. These jeans are—

Just stop talking, he said. I don't give a shit about the dance, okay?

Why should I stop talking? I said. How can I explain things if I don't talk? I can't move in these stupid pants and—

Why don't you just go sit in the corner and breathe, he said.

What? I said. That's kind of a dumb thing to say when—

There was a knock at the door and I grabbed my dress and put it back on and whipped off the sunglasses and went to see who was there. It was Miguel. He was leaning against the door frame, smiling and shy in his skinny black jeans and giant white sneakers.

Crap! I said. I forgot about cooking. I saw this fire in my yard and had to . . . I'm sorry. I'll be right there. Is Aggie still at the house?

No, no, I'm the one who's sorry, Irma, said Miguel. I don't mean to bother you. He looked around me and into the house.

No, no, it's fine, I said. But is Aggie still there?

Diego asked me to come, he said. Aggie is there, yes, she's fine. She's learning how to juggle devil sticks.

Jorge came to the door and I introduced him to Miguel in Spanish. Then Miguel left and Jorge closed the door and said. So, Irma, who the hell is that and what the hell is going on?

As questions go, they were good ones. Jorge took off. Jorge's gone again. I tried to tell him that my father was threatening to sell the house and I'd need to have a place to live, preferably with him, he was my husband, maybe we could live with his mom in Chihuahua city, I could sell cheese, I could get a job, I could learn to dance, but Jorge said those were just words.

Well, then this is just a situation, I said. And you're just a man.

You don't even know how to argue properly, said Jorge.

Well, I think your age is starting to show, I said. You didn't even fix the generator.

What do you mean by that? he said. We're the same fucking age. You're just saying stupid things to keep me here.

Why would stupid things keep you here? I said. I want you to stay. You're my husband. You're supposed to stay here. I'm probably stronger than you are.

What is that supposed to mean? he said. I was running along beside the car now. He was leaving.

I was yelling. Why do you want to know what everything means? I said.

Take your hand off the wheel, he said. Irma. Please.

I ran for a long time, like a dog, like Oveja. Stupid. I was stupid. But not stupid enough to keep Jorge from leaving. I had options. I could have stood perfectly still like the Tarahumaras, and waited. But all I wanted was to run. I fell a few times and ripped my new jeans, stovepipes the label said, no wonder they were so stiff, and scraped my legs and got back up to run some more. When I stopped to catch my breath I realized I was on the road in front of my parents' house and the lights were on and I could see my mom in the kitchen and it looked like she was cutting something with a knife and she kept looking down and then up and then down again and I guessed she was giving some bits of food to my little brothers. But they were too short for me to see them in the window and she was talking to them too. She was out of bed. I wondered if she was okay. Then I turned around and passed my house, mine and Jorge's, and there was nobody in the kitchen, nobody handing anybody anything. I finally made it to the filmmakers' house and walked right up to the front door and knocked my head against one of those plastic bags filled with water to keep the flies away and I punched it hard and broke it and the water sprayed out of it and drenched me and I didn't care, I opened the front door and walked in. Everybody, including Aggie, was watching TV and didn't really notice me but I said hello in a few different languages and then walked into the kitchen and yanked a pot out of the cupboard and slammed it onto the stovetop and hauled some food out of the fridge and turned on the tap to boil water and grabbed the sharpest, biggest knife I could find and cut up the vegetables and the meat and flung all the pieces into the pot to cook. Then I took some other pieces of meat and went outside and flung them at Oveja so he wouldn't forget that we were friends and then went back to my cauldron.

Irma, said Diego. He was calling me from the living room. He was shouting over the TV.

Sí, I said.

More rain is forecast for tomorrow, he said.

Hallelujah.

I heard Elias talking about some girl's rock-hard ass. He said it was so hard he could play "Wipeout" on it. He made some strange sounds. I heard Diego call Elias an idiot. They insulted each other's mothers, playfully. Then Elias started impersonating a woman. I threw more stuff into the pot and stirred so hard it slopped over the sides and onto the stove and made little hissing noises.

I could hear Aggie laughing, pretending to know what was going on. Go home, I said. Too quietly for anyone to hear. You should go home. Diego came to the kitchen to talk to me.

Oh my God, he said. Irma, I cannot believe this.

I'm sorry, I whispered. I'm not . . . This is ready to eat, I think. I pointed at the pot on the stove.

What are you doing? he said. He put his arm around my shoulder. What's wrong?

I don't know, I said.

Please stop crying, he said. Irma. Please?

He sounded just like Jorge, calm and sincere, when he asked me to stop screaming and chasing him down the road. He stood behind me. He put his arms around my waist and his chin on my shoulder. I kept stirring the slop I'd created hoping he wasn't expecting me to grind down to the floor right there at the stove.

I went outside and walked to the barn and sat down on the concrete pad and leaned against the door. Diego came outside and talked to me. He asked me how I was doing. He asked me what was wrong. He told me that his parents had died in a terrible car accident twenty years ago and after that his brother had decided to walk to America. He was fifteen years old. He left the house and started walking north and he hasn't seen him since.

Do you think he's alive? I said.

Yes, said Diego.

Why do you think that? I said.

Sometimes my phone rings and nobody talks, he said.

You think it's him? I said.

Yes, he said. I know it's him. I talk to him about things. Simple things. My life. My work.

And he never says anything? I said.

That's right, he said. He listens and then when he's heard enough he hangs up.

But why doesn't he want to talk to you? I said.

I don't know, said Diego. But it doesn't matter. It's not important. I'll talk to him and he'll listen. That's how it is now. Like a prayer.

Eventually everybody ate except for Marijke and José who were fucking in her room, according to Diego. She is very angry with me for making her ride with Alfredo in his truck, he said. So she is trying to make me jealous with José. I know her astrological sign well. Very intense. Have you ever been dumped by somebody you didn't even know you were dating? That has happened to me. It's surprising.

Oh, I said. So are you jealous?

Only a little, said Diego.

Where's Alfredo? I asked.

He went home to his wife and kids, said Diego. He and Marijke had a fight.

About what? I said.

Well, said Diego, from Marijke's body language I think that Alfredo made a pass at her in his truck. I spoke to him about it and he said it was nothing. He put his hand on her leg, like this, she could have been his sister, but she became inordinately angry. She said she wanted to break the truck's side-view mirror and use the shards to slice Alfredo's hand off and then throw his hand out the window for the condors to feed on.

But she didn't, I said.

No, said Diego. She hit him in the face. Now he's very mad and I'm a little frustrated with her, but don't tell her because I'm afraid she'll leave. European women are difficult, he said. They overreact. For instance, French women hate papaya. They say it tastes like urine. I know this. So, if she wants to sleep with José I don't care.

Diego went outside to stare at the sky. He needed rain. I wished I was a difficult European woman. It occurred to me that Marijke was the same age as my mother. Elias gave me a beer to drink when he saw that I'd been crying. It tasted awful. I had another one. We were outside sitting on the bench in front of the house because I didn't want Aggie to see me drinking beer. Elias taught me how to smoke marijuana from his vaporizer. He asked me if I wanted him to sing and I said yeah.

Frankie Valli or Van Morrison? he said. I don't know, I said. I don't care. Frankie Valli.

He started singing. He stood up and pretended to be holding a microphone.

I passed him his vaporizer. *Like heaven to touch*? I said.

Yeah, he said.

He sang for a while. You can't be in a bad mood if you're singing, he said. If you sing a song it's important that you sing the living shit right out of it. With this part of you. This part here. You should sing with me.

I don't know any real songs, I said.

How can you not know any real songs? he said. I thought about the songs I had vaguely known in Canada.

Your love is lifting me higher and higher, I said. Is that a song?

He told me he was going inside to finish watching the movie. I looked through the window and saw Aggie sitting very close to Miguel on the couch. Their knees were up like little kids. They had their arms around their knees. They looked like Russian dolls. I tried to think. I needed a plan. I closed my eyes and saw only vines and waterfalls. I got up and walked back out into the dark yard so I could see the stars a little more closely. They didn't give a shit about my plans. I was trying to figure out what I was going to do with Aggie and then I heard some scuffling and a familiar voice.

Buenas noches, chiquita, said Wilson. *Cómo estás?*

What are you doing here? I said. I can't believe you're back! Where did you come from?

I got a ride to Rubio and walked the rest of the way.

That's a long way to walk, I said. Are you okay?

Yeah, yeah, he said. A little tired.

Why did you leave? I asked.

That's obvious, isn't it? he said. Diego and I had a fight but we worked it out.

What were you fighting about? I asked.

I don't know, said Wilson. His recklessness. It makes me mad. I've worked for him before and we've had the same fight. He's a genius but he taxes me. I feel that he extorts from me. Painful feelings. And then I'm happy to be extorted. I don't know. I just want to make some money and go live in Paris or something for a while and write. Or just read, for like a month. Nothing else.

What do you want to read? I asked him.

Jung, he said. I want to read his journals and everything

else he's ever written. The way he understands the human mind. But not just the mind. Do you know him?

Let's go over there by the fence and talk, I said. It's darker. Irma, I told myself, try to make sense when you speak.

He walked ahead of me and I watched him. When we got to the fence I put my arms around his neck and kissed him. He smiled and leaned back.

Is it electric? I said.

I don't think so, he said, I didn't feel a shock. He put his hand on the wire fence and held it there for a few seconds. No, he said. Or it's burnt out.

That's good, I said. I kissed him again and took his hands and put them on my waist.

Do you have a girlfriend? I said.

No, but you have a husband, he said.

Yeah, I guess, I said. Would you like to make love right now? Or something like that? Do you think you could or are you too tired from walking?

Here? said Wilson. He looked around at more of the same. Grass, darkness, stars.

Well, maybe just . . . like, over there a bit, I said. I pulled him slightly farther away from the fence.

We lay on the grass and Wilson peeled my jeans off and lifted my dress up over my arms and then folded all that clothing neatly and put it under my head as a pillow. He sat cross-legged beside me and ran his hands lightly up and down my body. I barely moved. I stared at the stars, mostly. I looked at him once or twice.

Your knees are all scraped up, he said.

Those jeans are . . . they're called stovepipes, I whispered.

You have an on/off button, he said. He touched the mole in the centre of my sternum.

Aggie says it's Zacatecas, I said. If my body was a map of Mexico.

What's this?

Mexico City? I said. I smiled and looked away.

And this? He touched my eyebrow.

Juárez, I said.

You're beautiful, he said.

I like the way you walk, I said.

I like the way you moan, he said.

After all that, Wilson asked me if there was something I wanted to tell him, anything at all, because he would keep it a secret for me.

No, thanks, I said. I smiled. I put my clothes on.

I told you that I was dying, he said.

Is that a secret? I asked him.

Well, mostly, he said. Around here it is.

Okay, I said. Well, I used to have another sister.

The one who refereed your hockey games? he said. What happened to her?

Yes, her. She died, I said. In Canada. That's why we moved here.

How did she die? he said.

I don't know, I said. Nobody would tell me.

Are you sure she's dead? he said.

Well, yeah, I said. Otherwise, where would she be?

How old was she?

Sixteen, I said.

Did she look like you? he said.

She was far prettier, I said. And braver. I had this dream about her a while ago. I dreamt that I was in a van with a bunch of people, I didn't know who they were, and we were driving along the highway in Canada, in Manitoba, and we noticed that there was some kind of fair going on along the side of the road with different food stands and games and some rides and all that stuff so we stopped to check it out and we were walking around and a little bit beyond where everything was going on there were a few chairs so I walked over there because I felt like sitting down and then there was Katie, that's my sister, sitting in one of those chairs and she was a fortune teller! I was so happy to see her. She was happy to see me too. I had this date square in my hand, my mom calls it a matrimonial square, which was her favourite dessert, so I gave it to her and asked her how she was doing and she said great and that if I wanted she could read my palms. So I put my hands out for her to read and she held them and then she smiled and she looked up at me and that was the end of the dream.

Wilson took my hand. That's a good dream, he said. Jung would say it was positive, I'm pretty sure.

But that still doesn't mean that she's not dead, I said.

That's true, he said. Have you heard of the song of Nezahualcoyotl?

No, I said. I was thinking about Marijke. I was thinking about how she had asked me if I knew what the four-part cure was but said not to worry if I didn't because not worrying was part of the cure.

With flowers You write, said Wilson,
O giver of Life,
With songs You give colour,
with songs You shade
those who must live on the earth.

Later you will destroy eagles and ocelots;
we live only in Your book of paintings,
here, on the earth.

Can you say that again? I asked Wilson. I got him to say it five or six times until I had memorized it and could say it along with him in my head. We didn't hold hands when we walked back to the house but we had exchanged secrets.

The living room was empty except for Aggie and Miguel who had fallen asleep and toppled over in tandem, arms still locked around their knees, mouths open.

Who is that? whispered Wilson, pointing at Aggie.

My sister, I said.

She's alive! he said.

It's a different one, I said.

I touched Aggie's arm and told her that we had to go, we needed to do the milking, but she didn't move and she didn't open her eyes.

Ag, I know you're faking, I said. C'mon. You have to go home.

Miguel woke up and cleared his throat loudly and blinked and focused and stretched out his legs and high-fived

Wilson and said you're back. *Qué tal?* He got up and gave both of us a hug.

Está bien, said Wilson. He smiled and rubbed Miguel's head.

Aggie, I said. Get up. Now. You have to go.

I drugged her, like Roman Polanski, said Miguel, in slangy Spanish he thought I wouldn't understand.

Only way you'd ever get a girl, said Wilson.

At least *I'm* into girls, said Miguel.

Your sister doesn't count, said Wilson.

Aggie opened her eyes. We actually understand that, she said. Me and Irma.

Shit, sorry, said Wilson. Say sorry, asshole, he said to Miguel.

Yeah, sorry, said Miguel. We were just kidding around. Your Spanish is not very bad.

Aggie, I mean it, let's go already, I said. Get up. I pulled her arm and she yanked it back and nestled into the couch.

Why can't she just sleep here? said Miguel. She can use my blanket and pillow. Hang on.

No, she can't, I said. Miguel had rushed off to get his bedding. Wilson said he was going to get a beer, did I want one?

C'mon, Aggie, I said. Stop fooling around, okay? We have to go.

I told you I'm not going back, she said.

Yes, you are, I said.

I'll have a beer, please, she told Wilson. She asked for a pint but mistakenly rhymed it with *mint.*

What does she want? said Wilson.

Aggie, I said. Seriously. You have to go. I grabbed her arm this time and pulled her halfway off the couch.

Why are you so mad? said Aggie. Leave me alone. Let go of me.

I let go of her arm and she rearranged herself on the couch. I sat down next to her and stared straight ahead. I breathed deeply. I spoke to her in Low German. I made a promise.

She was quiet for a few seconds and then got up and said good night to Wilson and Miguel and foul Oveja, who had been let in for the night, and I followed her out the door and watched her walk down the road towards home, hers, and the bright yard light, and her own bed, and our parents, and I stood there for a long time because I didn't know where else to go. I stood there long enough to feel the chill of the night. The sky was a blanket of stars. Indifferent. I repeated the ancient song of Nezahualcoytl. I stood there long enough to hear my family singing. Why were they singing at two in the morning? I heard the high, creaky voice of my mother and the off-key but persistent voices of my little brothers.

Gott ist die liebe
Lest nich erlosen
Gott ist die liebe
Er liebt auch dich.

They sang another verse and I listened. And one more verse and I listened to that too. And then, finally, I realized what was missing, which were the voices of my dad and

Aggie, and I wondered why they weren't singing and then I knew and I ran to the house. My mother was wiping tears from her face and my little brothers were pale and stricken. They were sitting at the table holding hands and singing hard with the same energy you need to clear a field of rocks.

Where is she? I said. My mom pointed to the back of the house, towards the summer kitchen, and I ran over there and broke the flimsy hook and eye and ripped the screen door off its feeble hinge and told my father to stop hitting her, he was whipping her with a belt, and Aggie to come with me right then. Right then. My father and I looked at each other. His eyes were wild with fear and despair and he began to cry and he asked me to forgive him. He begged me to forgive him.

Gott ist die liebe
Lest nich erlosen
Gott ist die liebe
Er liebt auch dich.

That's a lie. My father hadn't said anything. But it's true that we looked hard at each other, briefly. I saw his eyes. I remembered Diego's words. I want her eyes to harm me, he had said when we met for the first time. I want her to be too big for her body, a living secret, squeezed out through here, here, and especially here.

FIVE

AGGIE AND I WALKED FOR A FEW HOURS, all the way to San Juan, a tiny village a few miles away. We didn't walk right into the town, that would have caused more problems, but to the frayed edge of it. It was still very dark, the village was silent, but we wanted to see the small, twitchy boy who'd built himself a very high unicycle and had to come up with ingenious ways of getting on and off it. We didn't see him. We hadn't seen him in years actually but we thought that life was messed up enough that night that it could happen. And then back to my place. When we got there Aggie asked me to remind her of the cold in Canada. How parts of your body go numb and all you can do is keep moving or you will definitely die.

I want that, said Aggie.

You want your body to go numb or you want to keep moving? I said.

I'm not sure, said Aggie.

I think that's normal, I said.

How would you know what's normal? she said.

That's a good question, smartass, I said, but I'm trying to make you feel better.

We lay side by side in bed. Aggie began to cry and I held her.

She finally fell asleep and my arm was trapped beneath her and I didn't want to wake her up so I let her lie on my arm all night long and in the morning when she woke up I told her that she wasn't going home again, that home had changed, that home, like thoughts, according to Marijke, were random patterns of atoms flying around and forever on the move. And I considered telling her that if thoughts and home were random patterns then actions were too, all actions, tender, desperate, lucid, treacherous ones and the promises we make and break, the secrets we share with dying Venezuelans, and the bruises and bleeding cuts on her back. All of them random patterns. And that they didn't mean a thing.

The rain that was forecast for today hasn't come. Diego is obsessed with the sky and is worried that if it doesn't rain soon his movie will be ruined. He is wondering, out loud, about alternative sources of rain. He's made a call to the *bomberos*, the firefighters, to see how much water they hold in their tanks and how far their hoses can spray it.

We're all at the table, eating toast and eggs and fruit quickly, about to leave for our next location. I'm not sure exactly where it is but I think it's a hill, somewhere south of here. I'm nervous about everything. Aggie can't go back home and she can't go to school because if she goes to school they'll make her go back home. Marijke is talking to Aggie about astral projection and while she talks she puts her hand gently on Aggie's cheek. Elias is talking about the constitution of the avocado which, when he bites into it, makes him feel like he's eating a baby. Alfredo isn't here yet but I think he'll meet us at the hill. I only get bits and pieces of information. I can hear Wilson telling Sebastian that his home is where he can do his art and I can see him listening and nodding respectfully. He doesn't want Wilson to leave again so he's willing to listen to his theories. Wilson smiled at me when I handed him his plate of eggs and toast and he whispered something but I couldn't understand it. Miguel has already left the table and is hauling equipment out to the trucks. Diego and José are reading something, a piece of paper, and Diego is pointing at it and talking very fast and rubbing his arm vigorously. The rebel spirit of my grandfather is directing this film! he said. José is perfectly still, like a kid playing freeze tag, waiting to be tapped. Neither one of them has spoken to Marijke, or even looked at her. Aggie has a cut lip and the red outline of a hand and all its fingers on her left cheek and Marijke hasn't moved her own hand from it yet. I think she's redirecting energy but I'm not sure. I'm nervous. I need to talk to Diego about getting paid and about Aggie getting paid too, if she's also going to help with the movie, but he seems so agitated right now and is already worried about how much everything is costing him so I'll wait until tonight when hopefully he'll have gotten the shot that he and the rebellious spirit of his grandfather are looking for and his life will be worth living once again. Now he looks a little sad. He's smiling at me wistfully, I think, as though I remind him of someone he once knew and liked.

We're at the hill and Alfredo still isn't here because of some family situation and Diego is upset. Elias has to listen to him while Diego explains that when he is on a plane and thinks that it might crash or when he's in a car and it's about to veer off a cliff he doesn't think about his family. He thinks about his film. How he has to finish his film because it is his duty to finish his film. That's how he thinks. He picks up a stick and says it has as much meaning as his own unborn child and then throws it far into the scrubby bushes.

I hate meaning! he says. Why is everyone searching for meaning? Elias stands and listens to Diego. He looks at the sky and nods, as though God is telling him it's okay, Elias, my son, be patient, Diego won't be angry forever, just listen for a little longer.

Aggie and I have been hauling stuff up to the top of the hill. Fruit, juice, water, granola bars. We're wearing cowboy boots to protect us from the snakes. Marijke is sleeping in one of the trucks which are parked at the bottom of the hill and probably stuck in the mud. Her legs are protruding from the passenger side window. She doesn't have to be here today for this shot, she's not in it, but she didn't want to stay at the house all by herself because it makes her feel like she's dead. José the producer has gone back to Mexico City with some of the reels of film. Everyone is gaunt and exhausted. It's so hot out here and we're so high up and it feels like the sun is punishing us for trespassing.

This is another shot of a kiss. A woman is here from Cuauhtémoc to kiss Alfredo who finally showed up. She was supposed to be a Mennonite from Campo 6.5 but Diego couldn't find a local woman willing even to pretend to be Alfredo's lover so he's using this pale Mexican substitute. They've tied her hair back and put her in Mennonite clothes and moved her head over to the left for the shot so that it's more of Alfredo's face and less of hers that will be visible. They're about to be passionate on top of this hill.

Sebastian, the soundman, is giving Alfredo more lessons in kissing. I'm trying to learn too. I see that it might work to put my hand on the back of Jorge's neck and then move it slowly up towards his hair. Diego is telling Alfredo to infuse this scene with love and tenderness, to spread his passion over every inch of the shot softly and smoothly like mayonnaise. He is encouraging Alfredo to think of something romantic to say to the woman. Words are lubricants, Alfie, he's saying. Alfredo is squeezing his eyes shut and seems to be thinking hard of what that could be. Aha, he's got something good. He opens his eyes and points them, smouldering, at the woman and says, I'm not indifferent to you.

Diego is screaming. Not indifferent? he says. Not *indifferent*? He can't stand this life anymore and has wandered away to find a branch to hang himself from. From a distance we can see him still waving his arms around and pointing at the sky and grabbing his head and picking things up and throwing them but we can't hear him. It's like he's playing charades and the thing he's been given to act out is *apocalypse.*

Alfredo says good riddance. He calls him Hitler and cracks open another vampiro. The others are wandering around and looking into the camera and up at the sky and getting things ready for the shot. Sebastian has kissed the woman from Cuauhtémoc at least seven times now, she's starting to giggle, and Alfredo is standing off to the side with a strange smile on his face, watching and nodding. Aggie and I are sitting on boxes off to the side, braiding grass and talking. Oveja is lying on the ground next to us, panting and farting in the heat. We can hear Diego asking his actors what they think is so fucking funny about kissing.

Alfredo has just pulled a gun on Oveja. They're official enemies. Before the actual kiss Alfredo is supposed to run, with ardour, to the woman and grab her zealously. Oveja saw Alfredo rehearsing this part and attacked him and Alfredo took his gun out of his pants and smashed Oveja on the head with it. Oveja backed off a bit and stood snarling at Alfredo who was yelling and ready to blow the dog to smithereens. He fired a shot into the air. Diego is now yelling also for Wilson to take the dog back down the hill and put him in the truck with Marijke. He's trying to explain to Alfredo that Oveja panicked and was convinced that Alfredo's intention was to kill the woman, not to kiss her, and how could he know otherwise, he was a dog. Are you not more rational than a dog, Alfie? Diego was yelling. He can't understand your actions but you can understand his because you are a man. Now stop this and put your gun away. Alfredo is threatening to leave again for good and Diego is swearing one inch from Alfredo's face. I'm going to put away my notebook and walk down the hill with Wilson and Oveja.

Aggie, I said, stay here.

Why? she said.

I'm going to the bottom to talk to Marijke.

I'll come with.

No, stay here. I'll be right back.

I wanna come.

No, stay here. I'll be right back.

I'm coming with.

We caught up to Wilson and Oveja and I spoke to him quickly and softly in slangy Spanish that I'd learned from Jorge and that Aggie wouldn't quite understand. Wilson asked me if he could put his arm around me while we walked.

Why? I said. Are you okay? I knew immediately that that had been a stupid question but I didn't know what else to say. Aggie walked ahead of us with Oveja, and Wilson put his arm around my shoulders and told me I looked pretty. I told him I couldn't do any more naked things with him like lying in the field without clothes on. I told him that

I felt so guilty and so bad and that I was terrified of Jorge finding out and killing me. Wilson said he could understand that. But, I said, I wanted more than anything to be his friend and to save his life. That came out wrong. He told me I was funny, that I couldn't save his life, but that we could be friends. It felt like we had come full circle, from one obvious point to another one just like it. I felt like I should have said other more important and unique things.

Wilson, I said.

Yes, Irma?

If you knew that this was your last day on earth what kind of story would you write? I asked.

Given that I would actually use that time to write a story?

Yeah.

I don't know.

Oh.

But it's a very good question.

I was rejoicing silently in my heart. I had asked a good question. And not only had I finally asked a good question, I had asked a good question of someone I was trying to be friends with as opposed to myself. A question that had breath attached to it, that had left my own body. Jorge told me not to ask questions, he hated them, he could always tell when I was about to ask one and he'd put his hand up and say no, please. Please. Was I betraying Jorge by asking a good question of Wilson?

We got to the truck and Marijke saw us and pulled her legs back inside through the window and smiled and said she had missed us and what was up? She got out of the truck and gave us all hugs. She looked tired. I wondered if it was true that she had been fucking José. I told her that we had had to take Oveja away from Alfredo. We all decided to have some potassium-replacing bananas and water and a rest before we trekked back up the mountain. We heard more shots being fired and I explained to Marijke that Alfredo was angry again.

Oh my God, she said in German, is he killing people?

No, no, I said, he's firing his gun into the air. He doesn't know how to kiss properly.

And that's what's making him so mad? she said.

No, it's the dog, I said. Oveja attacked him.

Marijke laughed. Wilson was teaching Aggie how to walk on her hands but it was a logistical problem because of her dress.

Come here you pig, said Marijke. Oveja waddled over to her. He was bleeding from where Alfredo had bashed him on the head. Marijke stroked his nose and said loving things to him in German which I didn't bother translating for him.

Then we heard Diego's voice shouting from Wilson's radio. He needed Marijke after all, he had changed his mind, he was so close to his perfect shot, and we were supposed to run up the mountain to where they were shooting immediately.

What about the sky? said Wilson.

It's perfect, said Diego. Send the girls now and tell them to move fast.

Diego said that Elias was running down the mountain halfway to meet Wilson with a reel of film that Wilson was to put under the seat in the truck and lock the doors. And

Wilson was supposed to give Elias a certain lens that he'd bring back up the mountain and everything was supposed to happen now, immediately! We were all about to head up the mountain when we saw Elias tumbling towards us and screaming in pain and the reel rolled along beside him on the ground. When Elias came to a stop Wilson kneeled beside him and inspected his leg and said he had to get him to a clinic because he thought his ankle might be broken and he radioed Diego to tell him what had happened and that his shot might not happen right now after all and Diego went insane over the radio and said we were done shooting for the day and possibly forever. He said that even if he'd been the original Creator he couldn't have conceived of a more incompetent film crew than the one he had. Wilson switched his radio off. We carried Elias to the truck and he lay in the cab while Wilson drove and Marijke and Aggie and I sat in the back.

Do you think it's possible to rot without even feeling it? said Aggie.

Rot? said Marijke. Like, decompose?

Yeah, said Aggie.

Without knowing? said Marijke.

Yeah, said Aggie. Like until it's a bit too late.

This conversation was being shouted at top volume against the howling wind. I looked at Wilson through the back window of the cab, through the rear-view mirror. I saw him mouth some words to Elias. I could feel my stomach writhe inside of me.

I took my notebook out of my pocket and made a list of troubling things.

Aggie is now my responsibility.
Aggie has to go to school, at least in the fall. But where?
We have hardly any money.
Jorge might never come back.
Our father is going to sell the house.
I have to get a map.
We'll have no place to live.
We'll have to stand silently by the road like that Tarahumara family. Forever.
I miss my mom.
I'm a bad wife.

I tore the page out of my notebook and threw it away into the wind and watched it float up and over towards Belize or maybe Paraguay. I opened my notebook to the first page where I had traced my hand and wrote the words *we live only in your book of paintings here on the earth* along the length of my ring finger. But it was so bumpy that none of it was legible and the letters looked like little worms burrowing under skin.

When we got to the clinic we unloaded Elias from the truck and carried him in. He was still groaning but we had stopped worrying about him. Marijke had gone off to wander around in the cornfield next to the barn. We had to walk past three deformed dogs to get to the desk where the nurse was sitting. Is this a vet or a clinic? said Wilson. It's everything, I said. The nurse was my quasi cousin. She had white-blond hair like Aggie's. Our great-grandpa had had thirty-one kids with three different wives who kept dying and we had all lost track of who was really who. She might have come from a different campo, like maybe 4 or 2.5 or something. She asked me if I was a Voth and I said yeah, you? She said no, Nickel, but used to be a Voth. I thought so, I said. She didn't need to ask what was going on or who these guys were. She told us to carry Elias right into the doctor's room and lay him down on the stretcher thing and the doctor would be there soon.

We heard some screaming. Finally the doctor came and told us to leave so that he could examine Elias and we went and sat outside on a fence to wait. We heard more screams coming from the barn.

What is that? said Wilson.

A mother, I said. She's having a baby in that other room next to Elias's. We were all quiet, even Aggie, listening to the woman scream.

I would just say no way and take the doctor's gun and shoot myself in the head, said Aggie.

We listened to the woman some more. Except for those screams there was no sound at all.

That's her husband, I think, I said. I pointed to a guy sitting in a truck with a bunch of little kids.

Why doesn't he go in? said Wilson.

They don't do that, I said.

Elias finally came hobbling out of the barn with crutches that were too small so he was hunched over like a little old man. Wilson walked with him back to the truck and Aggie rounded up Oveja and I went into the corn to find Marijke so we could go. It took me a while and when I found her she was sitting in the dirt, crying. I crouched down next to her and asked her what was wrong and she told me that she kept opening and closing her eyes thinking that eventually, when she opened them, she would see her son standing there in front of her. She was afraid she was going nuts in this fucking desert. She wanted to go back to Germany but she was afraid that Diego would kill her.

I can't leave now, she said. Or his film will be ruined. And then he'll kill me. It's simple.

He won't kill you, I said. That would be stupid.

He keeps saying he'll kill Alfredo, said Marijke. So why wouldn't he kill me?

He doesn't mean it, I said. That's how he talks.

I feel like I'm disappearing, she said. Look at me. Do you see me?

Yes, I see you, I said.

I put my hand on her shoulder.

We should go to the truck now, I said. Elias is done.

Sometimes I feel like my life is an invention, she said.

Well, I said, sometimes the only way I know I'm alive is when I feel the pain in my chest, because there's no pain in heaven.

What makes you think you'll be in heaven if you're not alive? said Marijke.

I held my hand out to her and she took it and I pulled her up off the ground. I was just about to tell her that she was as light as air but remembered that that was the thing she was afraid of and I kept my mouth shut.

We drove home in silence, collectively worn out from

the sun and our own individually wrapped pain. The crew had become smaller from being sick. Before it was hard to squeeze more than four people into the cab of the truck but now we could fit five. I asked Wilson to drop Aggie and me off at the end of my driveway. We had to milk the cows and then we'd come to the house to make some kind of meal for everyone. We got out of the truck without saying goodbye to anyone and found a box sitting in the middle of the driveway.

It's more of your stuff from when you were little, said Aggie. I was milking furiously while she took out the clothing from the box and held each little undershirt and dress under the light bulb that hung down on a cord from the roof of the barn.

Wow, this is hideous, she said.

You wore it too, I said. And it was Katie's before it was mine probably. Put it back in the box and then put the whole thing in the grain shed and come help me.

I wish Katie was here, said Aggie.

You do? I said. You never talk about her.

We're not allowed to, said Aggie.

Or it's just easier to forget, I said.

No, said Aggie. It's the hardest thing in the world to forget.

Yeah, I said. You can talk about her with me if you want to.

I don't want to.

You want her to be here, I said.

Yeah, said Aggie. But talking about her is useless.

No, it's not, I said. What do you remember about her?

Nothing, said Aggie.

Aggie, I said. That's not true. You do remember stuff. How can you want her to be here if you have no memory of her?

Well, you have memories of her, don't you? said Aggie.

Of course I do, I said.

And don't you want her to be here? said Aggie.

I said, I don't think your question makes sense.

How can you not know? said Aggie. Didn't you love her?

It's not that, I said. Of course I loved her.

Dad said you love your imagination more than real life, said Aggie.

What? I said. That's not true!

I'm just saying that's what he said, said Aggie. Maybe it's true. So what?

We should hurry, I said.

Why should we hurry? said Aggie. Are you in love with Wilson?

Just put all that stuff back in the box, I said.

At dinner Diego delivered a motivational speech to the cast and crew. He apologized for losing his temper on the mountain. He lost his composure and put his hand over his eyes and said he was sorry for putting us at risk. He asked Elias how his ankle was. Morale was low. Every five minutes something was going wrong. Diego had bought a bottle of tequila and was pouring shots for everyone, even Aggie. The Mexican woman he had hired to kiss Alfredo on the hill was eating with us too, along with two of her kids. I asked her in

Spanish if she was having an okay time and she said she was waiting to get paid. Alfredo was lying on the couch with a pillow over his face. Diego acknowledged that the going was getting a little tough, that conditions were difficult and that time and money were running out, but he had faith that it would work out in the end and that seven months from now we'd all be wearing beautiful *vêtements* and drinking champagne on a party yacht at the Cannes film festival where the world had come to be blown away by our efforts.

The art of making a movie is an exploding bomb, he said, and while it destroys it also re-creates.

I attempted to translate this for Marijke but she didn't really understand what I was trying to tell her. I had made her a giant bowl of green salad for her anemia and I kept pointing to it like all those pieces of lettuce were shrapnel or something and somehow emblematic of the creative process. I thought about grabbing the bowl and tossing the salad high up into the air and then picking up the pieces and returning them to the bowl but that just seemed dumb and by then Diego had moved on to compare the art of making a movie to anal sex (absurd and painful at first) and to the resurrection of Christ.

We need more blankets, said Elias.

And water, said Sebastian.

Wilson walked me and Aggie and Oveja back to my house. I whispered to him that I thought Marijke was having a hard time, that she was worried about going crazy out here.

Even with all her theories and voodoo? said Wilson.

Well, I said, this is the desert. He nodded and said that made sense. He said it took him a year to recover from one of Diego's films. He'll take your soul, he said. And then you have to spend some time afterwards looking for it.

Marijke doesn't want to look around for her soul, I said.

For the sake of the mind, said Wilson, it's very important to be able to communicate loneliness.

Well, I said, Diego wants Marijke to run down the road.

Run down the road? said Wilson.

To clear her mind, I said.

What did she say about that? asked Wilson.

Nothing, I said. I didn't translate it for her.

Why not? said Wilson.

I don't know, I said. I just don't think it's a good idea.

Because she might not come back? said Wilson.

That was the end of our conversation. He briefly touched my shoulder and I nodded once, the way a man would. We said goodbye. Then the night started in for real.

Aggie had gone to bed and I was sitting in the dark at the kitchen table. I was thinking about my family. Mostly about my mother. I tried to cheer myself up by remembering something from long ago. We'd had a phone in Canada. It was brand new. It had never rung. I remember answering it when it rang for the first time and giving it to my mom. It was my aunt Hildie. Katie and I listened to our mom with some astonishment while she talked to Aunt Hildie on the phone. Yes, my mom had said to her, you told me that. Yes, she said, I won't forget. Yes, she said, I agree with you.

I have to go now. Yes, she said, I'll remember. Now Hildie, she said, you know I'd wish for you to die. Then she said goodbye and hung up the phone and went back into the kitchen like it was no big deal. Katie and I were laughing so hard and our mom stared at us and asked us in German what had gotten into us and we asked her the same question. She explained to us that Aunt Hildie had chosen that day to worry about what would happen to her if she fell into a coma and she didn't want to be artificially resuscitated and wanted our mom to remember that.

Is it possible to communicate loneliness if the only person you're sharing it with is yourself? I looked around my little house and thought: Oh! Is that a prayer? I got down on my knees and I bowed my head and folded my hands and whispered dear God, bring me love. Bring me love. Bring me true love. Bring me love. I opened my eyes and got back up and walked to the bedroom and got into bed next to Aggie and waited.

I waited and waited. Then there was a knock on the door. It was my father and he was there to inform me that he'd just sold my house to his something something, some kind of twice-removed whatever, and that I would have to get out and take Aggie, if she was there with me, but frankly he didn't care where she was, and find other lodgings. Maybe we could get work cleaning for Mexican capos. If we were lucky.

I slammed the door in his face and listened. Nothing. I thought he must be walking back to his house. Then I heard some Bible verses being quoted and realized that he was still there.

But I have prayed for thee, that thy faith fail not, he said. And then louder, a practised crescendo I'd heard a million times.

And he said unto him, Lord I am ready to go with thee, both into prison, and to death!

I wondered if I should make some coffee or go back to bed.

And he said, I tell thee, Peter, the cock shall not crow this day before that thou shalt thrice deny that thou knowest me!

I couldn't find my canister of coffee. I let a cupboard slam by accident and swore. I didn't want Aggie waking up.

Then he demanded that I let him into the house. I didn't say anything. He started yelling and Aggie eventually came out of the bedroom and together we stared at the door.

It's Julius Voth, I said.

Don't let him in, she said.

Then we heard another voice.

Who's that? said Aggie.

I think it's Diego, I said.

Our father asked him what he was doing there and Diego told him that he'd been outside staring at the sky, looking for signs of rain, and had heard yelling coming from my yard and then had started to wonder what was going on and if I was all right.

Well, now you can leave, said my father, and stay out of our business.

I will, said Diego, but why don't you go home also.

You will not tell me what to do on my own property, said my father.

Aggie and I sat silently at the table waiting for it all to end. It took a while. Arguments between two visionaries are lengthy, I learned. One of these men will be dead soon, I thought. While they argued Aggie made shapes on the table with flour. Tiny words, then bigger, like an eye chart. And hearts and clouds and cacti and planets. I went far away in my head, back to Canada, to snow, to forts, to ammunition that could melt, to red wrists from sleeves on parkas that were too short, to eyes frozen shut with ice.

SIX

MARIJKE HAS TO DIE TODAY. It's a little bit out of sequence but Diego is in a hurry to finish the shots that require the co-operation of the Mennonites. The other ones, the ones of nature or whatever, he can do elsewhere, somewhere down the road. My father has put a bounty on Diego's head, according to Diego. That if he

> doesn't take his filthy pornography-producing crew who live like pigs and rape his daughters and leave immediately he will end up with a bullet in his brain. Diego has also threatened my father with swift justice if he does anything to prevent him from finishing his movie. I don't know if I believe it.

I asked Diego when I'd be paid for my work and he said tomorrow. He said first he had to pay the cops to let Carlito go.

Carlito Wiebe? I said. Diego said yeah, Carlito Wiebe. Diego had hired him to play Alfredo's friend but Carlito was busted at Campo 4 for some kind of drug thing and was in jail at the moment. How much will it cost? I asked him.

Four thousand pesos, he said. Plus the cop wants a part in the movie.

Diego told me not to worry. He asked me if my father was insane and I said oh, do you mean Julius Voth? And he said yeah. Then he apologized for talking that way about my father. I told him Aggie and I had to get out of the house, that my father had sold it to somebody. Diego told me that Aggie and I can live in the house with the crew. He said Marijke would like it and the presence of females might keep her from wigging out.

On the way to the death scene location we stopped to quickly film a scene where Alfredo and Marijke talk in the car. Alfredo is supposed to tell Marijke that he just can't stop loving that other woman or whatever, and Marijke is supposed to ask him why he doesn't want to be with her,

Marijke, anymore. I leaned into the passenger side window of the car and told Marijke that this time she'd be looking right at the camera. She wasn't really talking to Alfredo but it was supposed to look like she was. Alfredo wasn't there. She was talking to a camera that was on top of Miguel's stomach. Miguel was lying down, sort of, driving the car with the camera on top of him. He could barely see over the dashboard. Elias and Sebastian and Diego sat in the back seat.

Tell her to look right into that spot just above the lens, said Diego. To count in her head to ten and then to talk to it as though it were the love of her life.

I told Marijke in German to count silently to ten and then to ask the spot just above the lens why he doesn't want to be with her anymore. Marijke nodded.

And then, I said, ask is it because my vagina is so big after having all these babies?

This time I had gone too far. Marijke smiled and said I must be joking. Diego wouldn't have written that. Was it for real? Okay, well, no, I said, but it's more interesting and don't you think it's kind of the truth?

We can't wreck his movie with things like that, said Marijke.

Nobody seeing the movie will understand, I said. So what difference does it make?

It's not true to my character, said Marijke. I mean her character.

What character? I said. She's a prop for Alfredo's dark night of the soul. For his excruciating existential dilemma. She's barely breathing.

Did Wilson say that to you? said Marijke.

Yeah, I said. Don't let Diego take your soul.

What are you talking about?

Oh, I don't know, I said.

Suddenly I was exhausted. Diego told us to hurry. He asked me if Marijke was sure of her line and I said yes.

Then let's roll, he said.

Miguel began to drive the car, haphazardly, down the road. It was obvious that he couldn't see where he was going. I stood and watched them leave. I counted silently to ten and then saw Marijke turn her head to the camera, her husband, to speak to him with a broken heart. I watched them disappear into dust. Then they came back and left again and came back and left again and kept doing that for a while until Diego had his shot. He and all the others huddled around the little viewing thing that showed them what they had on film and nodded in approval. Beautiful. Perfect. Wilson would take the rushes today and fly them to Mexico City before they could be destroyed by my father.

Are you coming back? I asked him.

Yes, he said.

We were tearing to the house so that Diego could talk to Alfredo again. The death scene was postponed because my father had told everyone in church that if they co-operated with Diego they might as well book themselves a window seat to hell and enjoy the ride. He told them that Diego was stealing their women and perverting the will of God. He'd also made his position clear in more tangible ways, according to Diego.

What does that mean? I asked him.

Nobody in the area will do business with the agents of Satan, he said. Alfredo had radioed Diego to tell him that he had gone into the store to buy cigarettes and had had to pay twice as much as he normally would. Same with his vampiros. And the Wayfarer's Inn wouldn't serve him at all. Alfredo told Diego he was done. He couldn't take the pressure anymore. This really was it for him. Diego told him to meet him at the house. He sent Sebastian off to the businesses with some more money and a heartfelt plea to allow him to make his art. He told Sebastian to tell as many people as he could that the premiere of the film would be held in Campo 6.5 and everyone would be welcome, young and old, and it would be beautiful and sacred and true to the gentle and forgiving character of the Mennonite people.

It sounds like a war, said Aggie.

That's exactly what it is, said Diego.

When we got to the house Alfredo was standing in the middle of the yard with his wife and my father. Diego jumped out of the truck and walked quickly over to them.

Let's go in the house, I said to Aggie.

No, I want to hear what they're saying, she said.

Aggie, I said. Let's go in the house.

No, I'm going to wait here. You go.

He might drag you back home, I said.

He can't, she said. Can he?

Of course he can, I said. Come into the house already. We'll have Oveja.

We walked past Diego and Alfredo and his wife and our father. Oveja barked at them and I told him to shut up.

Don't look at him, I said to Aggie. Don't act scared.

I'm not scared, she said.

Our father said something to us, something I couldn't understand. If it was a harsh word he said it with a catch in his throat, like he wasn't convinced. Or that may have been my imagination. Tenderness bleeding like sap through bark. Maybe not. Then he said something to Diego.

It's not your property, he said. It doesn't belong to you.

I'm renting this house, said Diego, and the land that it sits on. So leave now, please. We have work to do.

Whosoever shall seek to save his life shall lose it, said my father. And whosoever shall lose his life shall preserve it.

Pardon? said Diego.

I tell you, said my father, in that night there shall be two men in one bed. The one shall be taken and the other shall be left.

C'mon, Aggie, move your ass, I said. Let's go inside.

Two women shall be grinding together, said my father. The one shall be taken and the other left.

Irma, said Diego, what is he saying to me?

I mumbled a few words, nothing really, and pushed Aggie towards the house.

Two men shall be in the field, said my father, and the one shall be taken and the other left!

All right, said Diego, I think I understand now. But—

And they answered and said unto him, where, Lord? And he said unto them, wheresoever the body is, thither will the eagles be gathered together.

Okay, said Diego. Okay. His hands were up to say stop, please, stop.

Then Aggie and I were in the house and couldn't hear any more of what they were saying. We watched them from the kitchen window. Elias and Miguel had showed up and were standing out there too, looking up towards the sky and clearing their throats. Then Wilson came into the house and said that he had to go right then to the airport with the rushes. He was carrying them and a tiny stuffed backpack.

Can you take Aggie with you? I said.

What? he said. I don't think so. Why would I do that?

Why not? I said. She can help carry things.

Irma, I don't think that's a good idea, he said.

Why not? I said.

Well, he said, it just doesn't make any sense.

So? I said.

I had started to shake slightly, a bit of old-fashioned trembling, but I was trying not to let it show. Then Diego came into the house and told Wilson to bring back two or three more guys from Mexico City, and to explain to José, the producer, about the money. He spoke so quickly I couldn't understand exactly what he was saying.

Irma, said Diego, walk with Wilson to the truck and take Oveja. And then come back into the house.

No, I said. I don't want to leave Aggie in the house without Oveja, I said.

Just to get the rushes to the truck, said Diego, and then bring the dog back inside. Go now.

Oveja and Wilson and I went outside and walked to the truck, past my father and Alfredo and his wife and some of the other crew guys. Wilson put the reels of film and his backpack on the front seat and got into the truck and said he'd see me the next day or the day after and Oveja and I walked back, past all those people who were just looking at us and not talking, and into the house. Then Diego went back outside and said something to Elias who slowly walked away towards the other truck. Diego kept my father talking for a long time. Elias parked the other truck behind my father's truck so he couldn't drive away and then he came into the house to get a beer and take a deep breath.

What's going on? I said.

Diego doesn't want your father to go after Wilson and steal the film before he can get to the airport in Chihuahua. So I had to block his truck.

I looked out the window at my father standing in the middle of a circle of young filmmakers. Alfredo and his wife had gone to stand in the shade by the barn. His wife had a small, tough body and a huge smile with one dead tooth, and gold-green eyes. I imagined Diego saying cut and everyone going back to their real lives. I stared at my father from behind the windowpane. I knew he was getting tired, that his back was hurting him. He couldn't stand for very long because of the three-inch lift he had built onto the sole of one of his shoes after the doctor told him he had some kind of scoliosis that had twisted his spine into the shape of a snake. I didn't want him to hold his hands out that way, palms up, or to wipe the sweat off his forehead with the back of his hand and I didn't want to see him stammer for the Spanish or English words that would add to the sum of his rage.

He won't do that, I said.

What won't he do? said Elias.

He won't chase Wilson, I said. That's stupid.

You never know, said Elias. There's a black . . . there's a black storm . . . no?

Yeah, I said.

Moving like this in circles, he said. Inside. He can't control it.

Yeah, I said. Tornado.

Yes, said Elias. A tornado doesn't know what it's doing. He started to spin around the room intentionally bumping into chairs and walls and kitchen appliances.

I know, I said. You're a tornado.

We should play music, he said.

He put on some music that would drown out the voices from outside and Aggie and I watched our father and Diego argue to the beat of something called cumbia. Slowly everything became dreamlike and soft in the dying light. Aggie got bored and started making pictures on the wall with the green tape Diego used to indicate to the actors where they should stand. I heard Elias talking on his cellphone. He was excited that he finally had service here on the moon and he was walking around the house trying to make it last. Can you hear me now? I heard him say in Spanish. How about now? Is this better? He lost his connection. Then he swore. *Puta.* That was my girlfriend, he said. She just agreed to give her body parts away to a hospital or something like that.

That's pretty nice, I said.

She prefers to give her body to science than to me, said Elias.

Well, science is science, I said. I didn't know what we were talking about.

That's true, he said. It's precise and useful. How can I compete with science?

I didn't know if he was being serious or not. I told him she'd probably change her mind when she realized how much energy would be involved in donating body parts.

No, Irma, she'd be dead, he said, it would be afterwards.

I am living beneath sea level in a basement apartment in Vancouver, ostensibly taking courses in fine arts and Marxism, I said to myself. It was a line from a letter my cousin had sent to my older sister Katie way back one hundred thousand years ago in Canada. You should join me. You'll like it here! Sometimes I recite these ancient lines to myself when I don't know what to say because I always feel my eyes open up a bit afterwards, maybe even shine with something like excitement or guilt, or like pilot fish. Ostensibly taking courses in fine arts and Marxism, I say to myself. You should join me. You'll like it here.

Diego came into the house and told Elias to turn the music down. My father was alone in the yard, standing close to a shadow cast by the barn. He could have moved into the shade but he didn't. Alfredo and his wife were gone. Diego told me he wanted to speak to me privately in his bedroom and I followed him down the long hallway that used to belong to my cousins and through the door with the upside-down cross and into his room. He had bottles of what looked like urine lined up against one of the walls. He had piles of books and a very neatly made bed.

Please sit, Irma, he said. I sat on his bed and he sat next to me and put his hand on my shoulder. Aggie has to go back, he said. I promised your father I'd make her go back. If she doesn't go back he'll call the police and the newspapers in Mexico City and tell them I've kidnapped her.

She can't go back, I said. I promised her she wouldn't have to.

She has to go back, said Diego, or I won't be able to finish my film.

I know, I said, but she can't go back.

And when I'm finished making the film then I'll make sure that you and Aggie are safe.

How will you do that? I said.

Don't worry, he said, I'll find some way.

He's not really going to call the police and newspapers in Mexico City, I said.

How do you know? said Diego.

And who cares if he does? I said. You'll tell them you haven't kidnapped her and that'll be the end of it.

That's not really the point, said Diego. He wants her back in his house. And if she doesn't go home he'll fuck up the production.

No, I said. She can't go back.

Irma, said Diego, she has to go back. Please. I'm begging you now. Please tell her to go home.

I can't tell her anything, I said. She doesn't listen to me.

Then I'll tell her, said Diego.

No! I said. Please don't.

Diego and I stopped talking and stared at the line of books he had on the little shelf above his bed. We looked at those books beseechingly, as though they were UN peace workers sent to help us negotiate our impasse. I imagined them rearranging themselves on the shelf to spell out some cryptic answer, a solution, but they didn't move an inch.

Tell my father that Aggie is sleeping right now and will go home in the morning, I said.

She's in the kitchen playing cards with Elias, said Diego. Your father can see her through the window.

Tell him she's sick with parasites, I said.

Irma, said Diego, she's sitting in the kitchen and—

And that she can't infect our mother or she'll lose the baby. Worms will eat it from the in—

That's ridiculous, Irma, said Diego. You know it is.

Tell him it's like a quarantine.

He won't believe me, said Diego.

Then tell him Oveja has to go with her, I said.

No, said Diego. We need Oveja here and besides, your father will just shoot him if Aggie brings him home.

You said we could live here with you, I said.

I know, said Diego. That was before.

Well, then I'm quitting, I said. I can't work for you anymore. If you send Aggie home you'll lose me too.

You have no place to go, said Diego. He looked at me kindly, steadily, like a cop who's just busted a kid for a very minor offence, like it hurt him a little bit but the evidence was there and it was irrefutable.

I need to get paid, I said. I need to get my wages.

Yes, said Diego, that is correct. You're right. Wilson will bring your money back from Mexico City in one or two days. I promise. I radioed José about it.

I got up and left Diego's room and walked down the long hall and through the kitchen, past Aggie and Marijke and the others, and out into the yard to my father who was now standing by himself in the half-light, waiting. He was in the same spot. He could have moved over and leaned against the wall of the barn. He could have held his arms out as I approached him. He could have kept us all in Canada and shape-shifted with the times. He could have been a million things.

Let Aggie stay with me at my house tonight, I said. I need her to help me pack my things up and clean the stove and fridge and stuff before you change the locks. When we're finished I'll send her straight home. For good. And I won't bother you again.

My father looked so tired. Daughters, I imagined him saying to himself. Who are these people?

You can do those things alone, he said.

But I can't do them and the milking too and have it all done by the morning, I said.

I don't need you to do the milking anymore, he said. I've arranged for Klaus Kroeker to do it from now on.

Well, I said. I could hear a few soft strains of cumbia playing in the house. The stars mocked me, even the puny one all on its own in Texas, four hours to the north.

I thought: I've run out of words. I have nothing. I've failed. My father was quiet, waiting. He could stand and wait it out, wear me down. He could stand forever like the

Tarahumara family on the side of the road. I could learn about this. I touched my forehead, the space between my eyes, the source, according to Marijke, of my energy and my light.

Please? I said. That was all I had, apparently, nothing but a dim flicker. Just the one low-beam request for mercy. I looked down at the ground. I covered my face with my hands. My eyes burned and tears fell. I got down on one knee, then the other, and prayed quietly at my father's feet. When I was finished I opened my eyes and he was gone.

I need to use one of the trucks, I said.

Why? said Diego.

I'll bring it back in an hour, I said.

Where are you going? said Diego. It's very late.

To see a friend, I said.

Is Aggie going home? said Diego.

Yeah, I said. I'll drop her off on the way.

I want to start shooting early in the morning, said Diego. Like at five a.m. We have to do as much as we can before everything goes to shit. Alfredo is giving me three more days before he walks. He says.

I know, I said. I'll be back in time.

And Marijke is losing her mind, he said.

She's fine, I said. She thinks she's disappearing but that's all normal, I think.

Aggie and Oveja and I were in my house, standing beside the kitchen counter, and Aggie was trying to get the tap to run but it wouldn't.

Don't worry about it, I said. He's turned off the water. Go to the pump and fill up some buckets from the barn and put them in the back of the truck and then meet me in the grain shed.

Yeah, but what if—

Aggie, I said. I know it's against your religion to do anything I tell you to do but you're going to take a break from your religion, okay, and you're going to do everything I tell you to do starting right now.

Are we in trouble? said Aggie.

Well, you know, yeah, I said. A little bit. Which is why.

Why what? she said.

Why I have a plan, I said. And then later on, in a week or so, you'll be able to once again refuse to do some of the things I ask you to do.

All things? said Aggie.

Just a few, I said. Just to keep your soul from disintegrating. Okay? Please?

Aggie sighed heavily and Oveja stared mournfully at her, his eyes a well of deep concern. He was also a rebel, a fighter, and understood the significance of what I had asked her to do.

Let's quickly eat something, I said.

There was some leftover shepherd's pie in the fridge that wasn't working anymore since the generator died and Aggie ate the meaty stuff at the bottom and I ate the top layer of potatoes.

Then we both went outside and Aggie went to the pump to get some water and I went to the barn and let out all the cows. I punched their rear ends and shouted at them and that got Oveja all worked up and he came running over and started growling and nipping and chasing the cows out into the yard and into the cornfields and onto the road. Aggie came back from the pump and put the pails of water in the back of the truck.

What the hell are you doing? she said.

Back the truck up to the grain shed, I said.

Why should—

Aggie! I said. Do it. Remember what I said?

I know but—

No, Aggie, you don't understand. Right now you have to shut up and do everything I say.

I know but—

Aggie! My God! Are you fucking insane?

Fine! she said.

I ran to the shed and stood on a bale and started hauling Jorge's boxes out of the rafters. Aggie backed the truck up to the shed and hit the corner of it with the bumper. I yelled at her to stop. She got out of the truck and came into the shed and I told her to start loading the boxes into the back.

What is this? she said.

Something for Carlito Wiebe, I said. Let's go.

Wait, she said, let's take Oveja.

No, I said. He's running around with the cows. We'll come back and get him after. And besides, Carlito has a dog too, and they'd just fight.

Carlito Wiebe was angry with us for waking him up in the middle of the night but then he saw what was going on and he became less angry. He took the boxes out of the back of the truck and brought them into his dingy little kitchen and piled them up on top of each other. He leaned on the boxes and said a bunch of things and I wanted him to hurry up and buy the stuff and give me the money so we could leave.

I don't have enough on me right now, he said.

Well, how much do you have? I said.

I don't know, he said, I'll have to take a look.

He went off into another room and Aggie and I stood there. She was yawning. Off in the other room Carlito put on some kind of cowboy music and we heard water running for a minute.

Irma? she said. Are you a narco?

No, I said. Shhh.

Jorge's gonna kill you, she said.

Nah, I said.

Carlito came back and said he could give me about thirty thousand pesos. I like that music, he said. Do you?

Yeah, said Aggie, it's pretty good.

It's a new band from Durango, said Carlito. The singer just got out of jail.

Jorge told me it was worth at least a million pesos, I told him.

He's wrong, said Carlito. He was just talking big. I'm going back to bed if you're not interested.

I'll give you thirty thousand pesos' worth, then, and take the rest back, I said.

No, Irma, said Carlito. I don't mean to be a hard-ass but you don't know what you're talking about. You don't even know how much thirty thousand is. Besides what are you going to do with it? Carry it around with you in the back of that truck?

Aggie cleared her throat and I looked into her translucent eyes for a second and felt weakness leave my body like blood.

Nah, forget it, I said. I'll find someone else. C'mon, Aggie, help me load this shit back into the truck. I yanked the back of her dress.

Hang on, said Carlito. Tell you what. I'll give you forty thousand pesos. That's a good deal.

Fuck off, Carlito, I said.

Fuck off, Carlito, said Aggie. We went into the yard and hopped back into the truck.

He's coming outside, said Aggie. What if he shoots us?

That would solve so many problems, I said. I rolled my window down and pointed my pen flashlight into his eyes. He put his arm up to cover them and I turned it off.

Sorry, I said. I had to make sure it was you.

Irma, he said. I don't mean to pry but what the heck are you doing?

I'm selling drugs! I said. Jesus Christ, man. What the hell do you think I'm doing?

Irma, said Aggie. You sound a tiny bit hysterical.

Does Jorge know you're doing this? said Carlito. Did he send you?

No, he didn't, okay? I said. Just, you know, whatever. Give me forty thousand then. I have to go.

Tell you what, said Carlito. I'll give you fifty. But promise me you won't tell anybody, especially Jorge, who you sold it to. And also, do you girls want a bag of oranges? We waited for Carlito to run into his house and out again with a big sack of oranges that he put into the back of the truck.

Danke schön, I said.

Bitte, he said. And may God be with you.

Thanks, Carlito, I said. And with you.

Count the money, I told Aggie.

No, she said. I'm afraid it won't be the right amount.

Oh, okay, I said, you're right. Never mind. I told Aggie what the next step was and she put her feet on the dash and said she'd like to make a comment if she could, something having to do with what she called the paucity of my business sense, but I said no. We flew back to our parents' house and went running in to tell our father that the cows were loose, that Klaus Kroeker, the guy he'd hired to do the milking, must not have known how to close the gate properly. My father grabbed his gun from the rack in the kitchen and put on his boots and told me and Aggie to help him round them up. His face was burnt bright red from stubbornly standing in the sun all that day. I told him that we'd take the truck and go over to the south side of the field, near the broken crop-duster, and stop them there. It didn't really make any sense but he didn't seem to notice and he left, swearing and bleary-eyed.

We went into our parents' bedroom looking for our mother and there she was with the top of her nightgown down and she was nursing a baby. We all stared at each other except for the baby who kept sucking and gurgling and then our mother said in a soft, quiet voice, girls, what are you doing here? What's going on? And Aggie said you've had your baby! Nobody told us! Shhhh, said our mother. She was smiling. Come sit here with me, she said. And then we both went and lay down on either side of our mother and her new baby for a while and we touched the baby very gently so we wouldn't disturb it from eating and I told my mother that we had some hard news.

My mother was quiet for a long time. I wanted her to say something. The baby fell asleep and my mother took her nipple out of its mouth and gently laid the baby down beside her so it was tucked in between her and Aggie and then she put the top of her nightgown back on. She asked me to move so that she could get out of bed and she asked Aggie to stay with the baby and I helped her walk to the kitchen because she was still sore from the birth and she asked me to sit down at the table. She sat down too and put her hands on my hands.

How are you, Irma? she said. She touched my cheek and my forehead. We were whispering.

I'm okay, I said. How are you?

She smiled and said she was okay except that I was holding on to her hand so tightly she thought it might break.

Does Jorge know? she said.

No, I said.

But he's your husband, she said.

I know, I said. She was quiet for a bit, staring at something invisible on the wall.

Are you cold? she said.

No, I said.

Are you hungry? she said.

No, I said.

Will you be brave? she said.

I'll try, I said.

I love you, Irma, she said.

I love you too.

I pressed my fingers hard to my eyes. I put my head in my mother's lap and she stroked my hair. My precious Irma, she said. Then she sang a little bit of this hymn we all knew called "Children of the Heavenly Father." When she was finished singing she was quiet for a minute. She kept stroking my hair.

Your braids need redoing, she said.

I know, I said.

But there isn't time now, she said.

That's true, I said. She tried to help me up. She whispered to me that I should kiss the boys goodbye, they wouldn't wake up, and she would talk for a bit with Aggie. I got up and went into the boys' bedroom and looked at them. Doft was buried under his blanket, his fuzzy little head just barely poking out, and Jacobo had thrown his covers onto the floor. I leaned over each of my sleeping brothers and kissed them. They smelled like hay and sweat. I wanted to give them something to remember me by but I didn't have anything. I kissed each of them again. Then I remembered the oranges and I went out to the truck and took two of them out of the bag and brought them back in and went and put one orange each beside my brothers' heads. I went back into the hallway and I heard Aggie and my mother talking in her room. I heard Aggie say hold me closer, Mom, squeeze hard. They were both crying. I walked back to the kitchen and waited.

When my mother came out of the room she told me she had a very big favour to ask of me. I told her I'd do anything for her.

Take her with you, she said, and don't tell me where you're going.

I am taking her with me, I said. That's why we're both here. To say goodbye.

I know, she said. I mean the baby. Take her too.

SEVEN

I WROTE A NOTE AND SLIPPED IT under the door for Diego to find when he woke up. I told him the truck would be at the airport in Chihuahua and the keys in the ashtray. I thanked him for everything and wished him well with his movie. I asked him to please forgive me for leaving the shoot early and for taking the truck and to give Marijke a hug from me and goodbye to all the others. And I signed it.

I drove fast, straight into the rising sun. Aggie held the baby and stared at her.

Does she have your eyes? I said.

It's hard to say, said Aggie. Just one is open. It's really dark blue.

Hmmm, I said.

I don't think she has any pupils, said Aggie.

Of course she has pupils, I said.

I don't know, said Aggie, I can't see it.

Well, that's just because her eye is dark blue, I said. She must have pupils.

What does a pupil do, anyway? said Aggie.

I don't know, I said. I was calculating the amount of time it would take us to drive to Cuauhtémoc and wondering if the *farmacia* would be open so that I could buy some baby formula and bottles.

You should know that by now, said Aggie.

Okay, I said, they react to the light. They dilate and contract.

So, said Aggie. If she doesn't have pupils will the sun just burn holes right through her eyes?

She has pupils, I said.

Maybe she's blind, said Aggie.

See if you can make her blink, I said. Or just move your hand around and see if her eye follows it.

Aggie moved her hand slowly through the air in front of the baby's one open eye and then the baby closed that one too.

Well, said Aggie, that didn't really work.

She'll be fine, I said.

You always say that, said Aggie. You're always saying everything is fine.

No, I'm not, I said. I'm not an idiot.

She has your fists, said Aggie.

What do you mean, fists? I said. Hands?

She's a fighter, said Aggie.

I'm not a fighter, I said. They just ball up like that on their own. Stretch them out.

Aggie took the baby's hands in her own and gently pried them open. The baby was trying to scratch her own cheek. Her hands were flailing around all over the place.

Don't let her do that, I said.

Do what? said Aggie.

Tuck her hands in under the blanket so she doesn't scratch herself, I said.

Isn't it strange, said Aggie, that Mom gave us all those baby clothes and now we have a baby but none of the clothes?

Yes and no, I said.

Are we going to look for Jorge? said Aggie.

I don't know, I said. I don't think so.

Wilson? said Aggie.

No, I said. I don't know where he is.

Well, you don't know where Jorge is either, said Aggie. That's why it's called looking.

I said, she's still kind of scratching herself. Tuck her hands in. Or hold them away from her face.

I didn't say goodbye to the boys, she said.

They were sleeping, I said. They're all right.

See, said Aggie, you're always saying everything is all right.

I didn't say everything is all right, I said. I said the boys are all right.

The motor on the truck was loud but we could still hear the mourning doves.

Dad will kill Oveja, said Aggie.

No, he won't, I said.

Yeah, he will, said Aggie. Stop saying stuff you don't know. I hate that. He'll kill him for sure.

Well, now you're saying something you don't know, I said. Maybe Oveja will kill him first.

What's he gonna do when he finds out the baby is gone? said Aggie.

Nothing, I said. He barely noticed her. Mom will tell him she had dengue and died and is gone.

That's it? said Aggie.

That's all, I said. You have to be buried quick with dengue. Mom will tell him she put her with that other one behind the feed barn.

What about a funeral? said Aggie.

Not worth it, I said. Dad will say a prayer at dinner and send her soul to heaven.

What does Mom call her? said Aggie.

Ximena, I said.

What? said Aggie. For real? That's a Mexican name.

Well, we're in Mexico, I said.

Let's give her a Mexican last name too, said Aggie.

Sure, I said. Molina?

Ximena Molina, said Aggie.

Or we could call her Miep, I said.

Ximena Molina Miep? said Aggie.

Sure, I said.

How will we feed her? said Aggie.

I'm thinking about that, I said.

It started to get a little cloudy and after about twenty minutes it started to rain hard. Finally Diego could shoot the scene he needed so desperately. Except that we had his truck. We were driving to the airport in Chihuahua city. I stopped at a *farmacia* on the main road going out of Cuauhtémoc and bought some baby formula and bottles and a bag of infant-sized diapers and a package of three sleepers and a blue box of moist baby wipes. I bought a beach towel with a herd of wild horses on it against a setting sun to use as an extra blanket for Ximena and a forbidden teen magazine and a Snickers bar for Aggie. When I got back to the truck Ximena was screaming and Aggie was trying to get her to stop.

You have to walk with her, I said.

It's raining outside, said Aggie.

Walk under that canopy for a bit while I make her a bottle, I said. I read the instructions on the formula tin and carefully measured out four level scoops of powder. I had taken care of babies all my life but until now my mother had always provided the milk. I added clean water and I shook the bottle and then I squeezed a drop of it onto the inside of my wrist to make sure the temperature was perfect. It was a little cool so I rubbed the bottle between my hands for a minute. I considered starting the engine and putting the bottle on it to warm up fast but I didn't want the plastic to melt.

Aggie came back to the truck with Ximena, she was still crying but not as hard and she'd stopped waving her arms around, and I took her and gave her the bottle and Aggie took her magazine and chocolate. Ximena spit the rubber nipple out several times and tried to scream but I kept putting it back into her mouth until she got the hang of it.

Aren't you supposed to boil those bottles before you use them? said Aggie.

Yeah, you are, I said. I shrugged. I wiped the bottle with a sterilized baby wipe.

When Ximena had finished her bottle I burped her and changed her diaper on the seat of the truck.

Look at that, said Aggie. Is that normal?

Yeah, I said, it's her umbilical cord. It'll fall off in a few days.

We should keep it, said Aggie.

Sure, I said. It'll eventually shrivel up, though.

How long will that take? said Aggie.

I don't know, I said. Marijke keeps her son's umbilical cord in a little pouch around her neck.

How far is it to the airport? said Aggie.

About an hour and a half, I said.

Where are we flying to?

I'm not exactly sure right now, I said.

How about Canada? said Aggie.

The world seemed spectacular and beautiful and calm, like the sacred heart of Jesus, as my mother would have said. The world we were leaving, that is. But I guess that's how the world works. How it sucks you in by being all beautiful just when you're ready to leave. Jorge used to get me to walk and talk with him when I was sad. He'd hold my hand and sometimes we'd skip all the way to San Miguel, the tiny village down the road, because skipping is stupid but exhilarating and it made us laugh. Words and movement, he said, would push all the bad stuff away. I tried it on myself. I was starting to think hard about my mother, wondering if we'd ever see her again, and I didn't want to cry in front of Aggie.

Are you thinking about Mom? I said.

Yeah, said Aggie.

Well, that was all we said. So much for words. And driving wasn't the same as skipping. So the bad stuff stayed in our minds and we both stared straight ahead through the dirty windshield. Ximena made odd noises like she was trying hard to fill the void but didn't yet know exactly how to articulate loss or, like Wilson had said, how to communicate loneliness.

We had Ximena and her sunset beach towel and diapers and bottles and stuff and the woman behind the counter asked us where our bags were and I told her we didn't have any. Well, we have a bag of oranges, said Aggie. The woman looked at the bag of oranges and frowned and looked at Ximena and frowned more. I told her I wanted to buy three tickets to Vancouver, Canada, or two if my baby could sit on my lap. She said we'd have to fly to Houston first, or Los Angeles, and then to Vancouver. She asked us when we wanted to fly.

Now, I said.

Do you have passports? she said.

———

We were sitting on the curb in front of the airport. I was nervous, worrying that my father would drive up any second. We had half an hour to kill before our flight to Acapulco. We didn't have passports. Aggie was eating an orange and leaning way over so the juice didn't dribble onto her dress. Some of it fell onto the asphalt and a bee spotted it just like that. And then a bunch of them. The baby was awake again and waving her arms around like a shipwreck survivor.

We've learned something today, haven't we? I said.

Is this my new school? said Aggie.

We'll go to the beach, I said.

We don't have bathing costumes, said Aggie.

Bathing costumes? I said. They're not called that.

That's what they're called at school, said Aggie.

Are those books from the eighteen hundreds? I said. They're called bathing suits now.

Bathing *suits*? said Aggie. That's worse.

Men call them trunks, I said.

Trunks? said Aggie. Why?

I guess you can figure that out yourself, I said.

We'll teach Ximena how to swim, said Aggie. Just throw her in like those hippies.

What hippies? I said.

I don't know, said Aggie. Hippies. They throw their babies into water right after they're born.

They don't throw them into oceans, I said. Here, hold her for a second so I can eat my orange.

A Mennonite family walked past us and we all stared at each other. The father nodded and the kids trailing behind him all dominoed into each other because they were staring so hard and that made us smile.

Aggie, I said, if anyone asks you if you're Aggie Voth, say no.

I told Aggie we should go inside and wait. I told her to hold Ximena while I went into the washroom to make her a bottle and she said she'd think about fake names for us while she waited. I looked at myself in the bathroom mirror. Sweat was pouring out of me. It was so sudden. My hands were shaking. I tried to make the bottle but formula was spilling everywhere and I was gasping for air. An older woman came out of a stall and stood next to me washing her hands. We smiled at each other. *Está enferma?* she said. *No, no, estoy,* I said. I washed my face with cold water and dried it with toilet paper that stuck to my skin in small chunks like porridge. I took deep breaths and tried again to make Ximena's bottle and this time I did it without spilling any. I remembered my father using the words *confronted by freedom* when he described the perverted temptations of the world and then I heard a loud voice reminding those of us flying to Acapulco that it was time to go.

I'm Fiorella, she's Button and you're Ham Hock, said Aggie. We were walking to our gate. We'd only be in Acapulco for two hours and forty-five minutes before we had to catch another flight to Mexico City, heaven and hell, according to Diego, but his world was defined by extremes. I was hoping we'd find some little street to live on that straddled eternities. If life was always going to be like this there was no way I'd be able to do it forever.

I'll skip all the flying stuff (because recounting it exhausts me almost as much as living it did) and keep this story about the things that happened to us on earth. Basically, it was a nightmare with Ximena Molina (Button) Miep. Vomit. Wailing. Flailing. Streams of shit. Screams of anguish. Aggie and I were both covered in puke and a little crazy with mortification. Eventually I gave up trying to comfort Ximena and focused on comforting myself with the knowledge that X., my newest baby sister, even with her unfinished features and ruinous needs, was a very honest person at least. So far. And that I had been given the task of keeping her that way. And so, if she needed to do these unholy things, then so be it. She was an ambassador-at-large, not appointed to any one country, but on a mission to represent babies, and I was her servant and facilitator.

We got off the plane in Acapulco and went outside and got into a taxicab and I asked the driver to take us to a beach. We smelled bad. We looked awful. Ximena had fallen asleep all wrapped up in the towel, soaked in sweat and with a sweet expression on her face that underneath it seemed to say fuck you all, I possess vital intangibles and when I learn to talk the world will know its shame. She was growing on me.

Aggie and I stared out the windows of the cab and tried as best we could to act like this was all just another typical day. The driver asked me if we had bags and I said no, not really, just this plastic *farmacia* bag with diapers and stuff in it, and he said okay, no bags, and shrugged. He smiled at us through the rear-view mirror the way Wilson used to when he was driving the truck and I was sitting in the back. He asked us in Spanish where we were from and I said Canada. He asked us if we were here in Acapulco for a holiday and I said yes.

Just the two of you? he said.

Three, I said. I pointed at Ximena.

No husband? he said.

Well, yes, I said. There is. But he's . . . I'm a widow.

The cab driver said he was sorry. He said he was raised by a single mother and it was always hard for her. She had cried secretly at night. It's not impossible, though, he said. He told me I'd be all right. It was a different world now, he said.

Which resort are you going to? he asked me.

Oh, I said. It doesn't matter. Just any one with a beach.

They're all on the beach, he said. Do you have the name of your hotel? Aggie cleared her throat and Ximena sighed in her sleep. Everybody started honking their horns at once, it seemed, and music was playing in every car and I was sure I smelled salt water, like we were all in some kind of parade.

Can I just tell you something? I said to the driver.

Of course, he said. You can tell me anything. He turned his music down and glanced at me through the rear-view mirror.

I don't know the name of the hotel, I said. We don't actually have a hotel. We're only here for two hours and forty-five minutes and then we have to go back to the airport to catch another plane. I promised my sister I'd take her to a beach. She's never been to one before.

The cab driver said he'd take us to a quiet beach that real people from Acapulco went to and we could eat fish tacos and drink mango juice and splash in the waves and lie in the sun to dry off and then he'd take us back to the airport, no charge. He was feeling generous, he said, and that he could use some time off because he'd been working for something like eighteen hours straight and he couldn't feel his ass.

Okay, I said. That sounds like a good idea. *Gracias.*

For real? said Aggie. I hadn't seen her smile like that in ages.

Les gusta este lugar? he said.

Sí, sí, I said.

Me llamo Gustavo, he said.

Do you trust him? Aggie asked me in Low German.

Why not? I said.

You don't even know him! she said. What if—

So what? I said. We'll scream if he tries anything.

Aggie reminded me in Low German that we didn't have any bathing suits. Ximena woke up and started kicking and punching. Soon she'd be into full-blown wailing but she was still just frowning and sputtering and quiet enough that the car horns and music everywhere drowned her out. She stared at me with one dark eye like a pirate and tried to claw my face. I held her to the window so she could focus her wrath on the outside world. I'm not sure she saw anything except for a blur of cars and buildings and sky.

Que bebé tan hermoso! said Gustavo.

Sí, gracias, I said. Babies weren't called beautiful in the campo. I put my ugly face next to Ximena's and together we looked at the city of Acapulco and I remembered the lyrics of a song I used to sing in church with my parents when I was a kid. *Beautiful words, wonderful words, wonderful words of life. Words of life and beauty teach me faith and duty. Beautiful words, wonderful words, wonderful words of life.*

Tell him we have to stop somewhere to buy bathing suits, said Aggie.

I told her that for some reason I was kind of embarrassed to ask Gustavo to stop and Aggie said it was more embarrassing to show up at a beach without bathing suits and she had a point. I liked her life theory of decision making—choose the least embarrassing option—and so I asked him if we could quickly stop at a shop along the way. Yeah, it was no problem, he said. He would hold the baby while we ran in and grabbed something. It was just a little beach hut along the side of the road that catered to tourists. Aggie bought a white bathing suit in two pieces. There was a gold chain around the waist of the bottom piece with a little fake combination lock and the words *RICH BITCH* in shiny gold letters across the top. Mine was yellow with a big blue anchor on it.

When we got back to the cab Gustavo was talking to Ximena about his childhood. I heard him tell her that she would have to be strong as the daughter of a single mother. My life is hard to lead, he said, but in the end there is happiness. That to truly know happiness is to know the fleeting nature of everything, joy, pain, safety and happiness itself.

Ximena was lying on the front seat glaring at him like a female prisoner with her hands all balled up into fists but at least she was quiet, entranced by his voice. Aggie and I got back into the cab and Gustavo told all of us a story about how he used to be a mailman in Mérida and one day he had just lifted the lid off a mailbox to put the letters in it and a bird flew out and it scared him so much that he screamed and fell over backwards and down the stone steps of the house. He lost consciousness and when he woke up he was in the hospital and couldn't remember anything. It took him six weeks to get his memory back and when he went back to work they told him that his job had been given to somebody else. He became angry and then depressed, too depressed to look for another job, and then his wife became frustrated with their poverty and left him for another man and took their son with her. He never saw them again but his son sometimes visits him in dreams and sometimes Gustavo hears him whispering into his ear while he drives his taxicab around Acapulco.

Just one little bird, said Gustavo. Ximena looked at him suspiciously. I picked her up off the front seat and we drove to the beach where the real people go.

Aggie jumped around in the waves and I sat in the shade with Ximena who lay naked on her sunset towel, churning and shadowboxing. She never stopped moving. I took a peek at my body. Not good, I thought. I was so pale and bony. I looked like a skeleton in the sand. Like something only an archaeologist would be thrilled to get his hands on.

Gustavo had brought us mango juice and fish tacos that he got from a man in a *palapa.* They were friends. When he handed me the juice and tacos he told me I looked sad.

No, I said.

No? he said.

Estoy un poco triste, I said.

Gustavo smiled and nodded. He turned for a second to watch Aggie in the water and he waved and she waved back. Then he pointed at my stomach.

Nice anchor, he said.

Thank you, I said.

Do you know something? he said.

No, I said.

My wife and I used to come here when she was big and pregnant with our son. I dug a hole in the sand for her belly so she could lie on her stomach. It made her so happy. Our little son was incubated in the cool sands of Patricio Beach. When she lay there like that with her stomach in the hole nobody knew she was pregnant.

Then Gustavo prepared what he called his beach station. It was an elaborate performance and there were many steps involved. He set up his beach chair, the long kind you can recline on, by adjusting the back of it so that it was at a perfect angle. He left for a few minutes and returned with a little plastic table that he stuck in the sand next to his beach chair. He spread his towel over the chair so there were no wrinkles and it hung evenly over both sides. Then he left again and came back with another mango juice and some fish tacos and a newspaper which he carefully arranged on the little table. He adjusted his sunglasses.

He re-straightened his towel. He kissed his fingers and pointed them at the sky. He lay down on his chair and then spent a long time wrestling his newspaper into submission against the wind. He was quiet for a few seconds, reading. Then he decided to reach for his mango juice and as he did that something snapped and his beach chair collapsed and he knocked the little table over and dropped his newspaper which went flying off towards the water in several sections, entertainment, sports and crime.

I hadn't laughed in so long. I couldn't stop. I tried to. Ximena stopped wriggling and stared at me. Gustavo swore and turned around to look at me. One of the lenses in his sunglasses had popped out.

You did that on purpose, I said.

I did not! he said. Now I have to start again!

He went through the same process again and managed to maintain his position on the chair for a bit longer before another disaster struck. This time seagulls surrounded him and one even landed on his stomach and he called for help. But I had seen him deliberately put little pieces of fish taco all around his chair to attract them.

Help me! he said. I'm being attacked!

I loved Gustavo. If I'd been his wife I wouldn't have left him just because he was feeling depressed and not making any money. If I was his little son I'd be in the streets looking for him right now.

Why are you laughing at me? he said. My God! Help me!

It was time to go back to the airport. After Gustavo's performance he had offered to watch Ximena while Aggie and I jumped in the waves together, holding hands like little kids and shouting at each other over the wind like we used to do in the back of pickup trucks. Gustavo gave Ximena a bottle while Aggie and I changed out of our bathing suits behind some trees near the *palapa*.

Look at this, said Aggie.

What? I said.

She held up her hand and there was blood on her fingers. She curled her fingers to make a claw and made a feral animal sound.

Oh, I said. You've started. That's okay.

I don't have anything, she said. We have to stop again.

I was counting the money that was at the bottom of the plastic bag we used for all of Ximena's stuff.

I guess that's it for me, said Aggie.

You'll get used to it, I said. It's just a pain in the ass.

Goodbye childhood, said Aggie.

Take this and put it in your panties, I said. I handed her one of Ximena's diapers.

No! said Aggie.

Fine, then bleed all over, I said. We had a little fight then. I was trying to count and kept having to start again. I turned my back to Aggie to give her the option of using the diaper after all without me noticing. I made a point of counting out loud, slowly, while she figured it out.

One minute you're jumping in the sparkly waves for the first time in your life and completely *unable* to stop laughing and the next you're shedding the useless lining of your uterus and smearing messages in blood in porcelain bowls and sandy beaches. Words of shame like I'm sorry about this mess and the smell and I don't know why the hell I'm crying on such a beautiful summer day.

At the airport Gustavo held each of us close to his warm body, his beating heart, and told us that if we were ever in some part of Mexico, I can't remember now which part, we had to go to the lake of echoes and that anything we said would be cannonballed right back at us clear as day. If you say, for instance, the name of the person you love, then the world will say it back to you as though it is confirming that it understands.

You can yell anything, said Gustavo, and the world will confirm it. You could yell *Vive mucho tiempo el muerto!* Or you could yell *Esto es una locura!*

We will, I said. If we can find it.

Or you could yell *Chivas!* he said. *El Rebaño Sagrado!* That's my team.

What team? said Aggie.

Soccer, I said.

The sacred herd, said Gustavo. You haven't told me your names.

I know, I said. I'm sorry.

I understand, he said. I'm a cab driver. Nothing surprises me.

That's good, I said.

No, said Gustavo, it's a tragedy.

We said goodbye to Gustavo. But then he said wait a

minute and he ran to his cab and took something out of his glove compartment and ran back to us and handed me a tiny photocopied picture of a boy.

Is this your son? I said.

Yes, said Gustavo, it's Raoul Elisandro Lopez Mundo. He's nine years old. If you see a boy who looks like this please tell him to contact me, Gustavo, at the address printed on the back. He turned the paper over and pointed at the telephone number and address in Acapulco.

Where did you last see him? said Aggie.

At home, said Gustavo, in Mérida.

That's so far away, said Aggie. What's the population of Mexico? Now that she had bid farewell to her childhood and all of its impossible dreams she had suddenly become ruthlessly pragmatic. Gustavo and I shrugged.

Millions and millions, I said.

How will we find him? she said. And hasn't he changed since this picture was taken?

I know, said Gustavo, that's true. That's all true.

It would be a miracle if we found him, said Aggie.

Yes, said Gustavo.

Aggie put the photo into our plastic bag of random stuff and we stood on the curb outside the airport and waved goodbye again. Aggie made Ximena wave too, by waggling her arm around like a rag doll.

We all fell asleep on the plane to Mexico City. I was trying to stay awake long enough to make a mental list of the things that we needed. They were all simple things: food, shelter, clothing, money, school for Aggie, a job for me and a babysitter for Ximena. I had wanted to get my notebook out of the plastic bag but I couldn't reach it without waking up my sisters. Aggie's head was on my shoulder and Ximena was curled up in my lap with her arms around an empty bottle. I imagined Jorge and Wilson on either side of me, stroking my hands and agreeing to get along. We were all smiling. We'll live together as an unusual family, said Jorge. We'll have an apartment with big windows, said Wilson. Or a lighthouse with round rooms, said Jorge. The last thing I heard was the voice of an older woman who was sitting behind me and talking to a young man. Where is the art made from intense personal necessity? she said in Spanish. He answered her quietly, whispering, and I couldn't make out what he said.

When we landed the three of us moved dreamlike through the artificial world of the airport and then out and into the real world of Mexico City and for the first time in a million years it occurred to me that my chest wasn't hurting and it was as though I were experiencing a strange, foreign feeling like bliss or something which meant that either I had died in my sleep on the plane or I don't know what.

Where would you like to go? said the taxi driver at the airport.

Aggie and Ximena and I all looked at each other for a couple of seconds and then I said well, I guess the Zócalo?

The Zócalo? said the taxi driver. No, you don't want to go to the Zócalo now. There are thousands of people there protesting. It's a zoo. Total chaos.

I know, I said. I didn't know what else to say. It was the only place in Mexico City that I could name and that was only because Diego had been talking about it on that day when we were stuck in the field waiting for the right kind of rain.

I won't be able to drop you off at the Zócalo, said the taxi driver. Or even close to it. All the side streets coming off it are jam-packed too. It's not a good idea to go there.

I know, I said. That's okay. Just as close as you can get will be fine.

He shook his head and peered at us through the rear-view mirror. I smiled at him. He looked worried. I imagined myself reaching over the seat and moving my finger gently over the ridge of his furrowed brow the way Marijke had done to me on the day we met.

We drove down wide avenues and narrow streets and past a park where men were hanging upside down from ribbons and spinning around a very tall pole, it must have been two hundred feet up in the air. The ribbons were wrapped around their feet so their arms were free to stretch out like wings or to hold on to tiny horns and drums which they blew and banged on periodically while they spun upside down way above the earth.

What's that? said Aggie.

A tradition, said the taxi driver.

We turned around and peered up at the men from the back seat window until we couldn't see them anymore.

It's not going to work, said the taxi driver.

What won't work? said Aggie. Her braids had come undone and her hair was wild and twisted around her head like a sun corona. She was beautiful in a deranged way and I was relatively calm after my nap on the plane and Ximena was still very much alive and we had seen men flying serenely through the air and . . . well, that was enough.

Obrador won't accomplish anything with his tent city, he said. Calderón is official and it's done.

Ximena started to cry, this was bad news for her, and I made a bottle for her in the back seat with the last of the milk formula and the clean water. Aggie stuck her filthy finger into Ximena's mouth so she'd have something (toxic) to suck on while I made the bottle. She gently caressed the tips of Ximena's ears because Oveja had loved it and so why shouldn't a baby.

Are you here to sell cheese? said the taxi driver.

No, I said. I mean yes. Aggie looked at me and rolled her eyes and muttered a word in Low German that meant something like emperor with no clothes.

Where is it? said the taxi driver.

The cheese? I said. It's with somebody else.

The cheesemonger, said Aggie.

Right, I said. I asked Aggie in Low German if that was another ancient word she'd learned from her stone tablet textbooks and she smiled and said nothing.

We're meeting the cheesemonger in the Zócalo, I said.

He's next to the cobbler, said Aggie. Across from the haberdasher.

Really? said the taxi driver.

Okay, I said. No. We're not selling cheese.

I just thought you might be selling cheese, he said, because of the way you're dressed. I thought you were *vendequesos*.

Not all Mennonites sell cheese, I said.

Well, I know that must be true, he said.

We walked for blocks towards the Zócalo, taking turns carrying Ximena. It was loud. There were people everywhere. It was getting dark. We stopped at a *farmacia* along the way and bought more baby formula, bottled water, pads, toothpaste, toothbrushes, diapers, notebooks, pens, a package of three boy's sleepers (part of her disguise) and a primitive stacking toy for Ximena that Aggie insisted on buying even though I told her she was too young to appreciate it. Then we stopped in a clothing store and bought jeans, T-shirts and hooded sweatshirts for warmth *and* style, according to the clerk. Even so, we still looked like idiots. We looked at each other and laughed our heads off. We left the store self-consciously, a little shy, like astronauts stepping out onto the moon. Somebody will rescue us, I thought. Somebody will notice we're missing and come and find us and bring us back home and be so happy that they found us unharmed and healthy. That might not happen, was my next thought. Then the third and final thought in this dumb trilogy was: Well. Okay. There was more sub-thought to that one but essentially I had made a decision. There was a sidewalk kiosk that sold knives and strollers so we bought one of each of those for protection *and* comfort, although Ximena was too small really for a stroller so we used it for our stuff and I tied her tightly to my chest with my old dress, and kept on walking towards the Zócalo with ridiculous grins on our faces in spite of being almost completely broke now and having no discernible future.

EIGHT

THE THREE OF US STOOD IN AWE at the edge of the Zócalo. I didn't know what to compare it to. Maybe a very large field of corn, every stalk a human being, or a desert night sky packed with stars, or a page in a notebook where every available space is filled with ink, words, letters and parts of letters.

C'mon, I said.

Where to? said Aggie.

Just follow me, I said.

What are we doing? she said.

I don't know, I said. Protesting.

Protesting what? she said.

I don't really know, I said.

It seems like we're just walking, said Aggie.

We sat down finally so that I could make another bottle for Ximena who had woken up starving and livid and with contempt for all she saw.

She's clawing out her eyes again, said Aggie.

Don't let her, I said.

Next to us was a group of young men and women banging on pots and pans and dancing and laughing and poking playfully at each other while they attempted to unravel some kind of banner with blood-red lettering. We stared at them. One of them yelled something incomprehensible into a bullhorn and the rest of them continued to dance around. Ximena was going nuts and Aggie was jiggling her a bit trying to calm her down while I prepared the bottle. The young men and women next to us started talking about the meaning of some English words.

The words *plangent* and *trenchant*, said one of the guys, they mean different things.

I've never heard of either one of them, said one of the girls. I think you're full of shit.

No, no, said the guy. One means incisive and one means sad or maybe reverberating but I just use them to mean HA HA.

The girl laughed again and Aggie and I looked at each other, confused. I thought the boy was in love with the girl. She mocked him and kissed him and laughed at him and jumped on his back. We continued staring. She reminded me of Katie and I wanted to say that to Aggie. I wanted to describe to her the way Katie rebelled, with jokes and smiles and affection and with some kind of tragically naive understanding that it would all be fine and even fun and definitely, ultimately, forgivable. But how do you talk about that?

Power was stolen in this case, said one of the guys.

Power is always stolen, said the girl. Again a huge grin on her face and kisses for everyone.

Here, feed her, I said to Aggie. I had finished making the bottle. I wanted to observe these people and make notes in my notebook.

No, you do it, said Aggie. I don't want her to throw up on me.

Use my old dress as a shield, I said.

No! I'm not gonna sit here draped in that ugly thing, she said. I'm going to look at stuff.

She started to walk away and I told her not to wander too far and to come back in twenty minutes. She waggled her ass at me. She didn't look back. She looked like a normal girl in those jeans and sweatshirt. I watched her walk in the direction of the National Palace, the place the seven Mennonite men came to a long time ago with grim hopes of making a land deal. I imagined her going in and saying hey! El Presidente! Time for a new deal! I fed Ximena. We looked deeply into each other's eyes while she drank. I liked the heavy, warm weight of her in my arms. I kissed her forehead and the motion made her lose her grip on the nipple and she craned her head around to my breast, her mouth open and searching for the thing she'd lost.

The jokey girl came over and sat down beside me. The boys were kicking a tiny beanbag or something around in a circle trying to keep it from falling to the ground. The girl told me she had noticed the three of us and was wondering where we came from. I was going to say Canada, but I said Chihuahua, the truth. She asked me if we had come to Mexico City for the protest and I said no, not exactly.

Are you tourists? she said.

No, not really, I said.

Have you been to Mexico City before? she said.

No.

There's a ruined temple beneath us, she said.

There is? I said.

It was once used for Aztec worship and human sacrifice, she said. She stroked Ximena's cheek with the side of her finger and made the sound we use to ward off rattlesnakes in the desert. Ximena stopped sucking on the bottle and stared at her.

Spanish conquistadors used bricks from the temple to help build their own capital, she said.

I nodded and smiled. They were like that, she said. Can I hold her?

Of course! I said. I handed Ximena over to the girl. I pointed at the enormous Mexican flag in the centre of the Zócalo.

I've never seen a flag that big before, I said.

Me neither, said the girl. She sang a Spanish song to Ximena who was eerily quiet and a little dumbstruck. Her tiny mouth was wide open like she'd forgotten there wasn't a nipple still inside it and she seemed unable to blink.

What's your name? I asked the girl.

Noehmi, said the girl. What's yours?

Irma Voth, I said. She's Ximena. And my sister Aggie is here somewhere.

Cool, said the girl.

Noehmi is showing Ximena to her friends. They're all crowded around her. They're taking turns holding her. Aggie hasn't come back from looking at stuff yet. When I took out my notebook Noehmi asked me if I was a reporter and I didn't know what to say so I smiled. So, you are? she said. No, I said. I don't think so. But you're writing things down in a notebook, she said. Why? I told her I wasn't sure. I told her I was making lists of the things I needed to do. Then I put the notebook away into the pocket of my new hoodie because I was embarrassed. Then, when Noehmi started to show Ximena around to her friends, I took it out again. I love my new notebook. I love the sound my new pen makes on the paper and the thickness of the pages. It terrifies me. There's so much to write about but I don't know where to start. I miss my mother. I wish I had something nerve-shattering to say. If trenchant and plangent mean HA HA then what's the point of any word? Just begin, I think. I have to find Aggie now.

We'll watch her, said Noehmi.

Are you sure? I said. She's extremely violent.

Absolutely! said Noehmi. We'll be right here. We're not going anywhere until there's a recount and Obrador wins. This is a peaceful protest, so Ximena will learn passive resistance from us.

I made another bottle for Ximena and gave it to Noehmi, just in case.

Can I ask you a quick question before you go? said Noehmi.

Sure, I said.

What was that language you were speaking with your sister? said Noehmi.

It's called Plattdeutsch, I said. It's like German, I guess. And we sometimes speak English and sometimes Spanish.

It sounds medieval to me, said Noehmi.

Yeah, I guess, I said.

What's your favourite? said Noehmi.

I don't know, I said.

English? said Noehmi.

I like it but Aggie doesn't know it very well.

What language do you dream in? said Noehmi.

English and Spanish, I said. Never Plattdeutsch.

Maybe that's because English and Spanish were the languages you learned secretly when you weren't supposed to, said Noehmi.

Is that what dreams are? I said.

I don't know, said Noehmi. She laughed. Nobody knows. Have you heard of lucid dreaming?

No, I said.

I'm reading this book called . . . *And Other Problems in Waking Life*, she said.

Other problems besides what? I said.

Sadness, loneliness, anxiety, depression, fear, despair, numbness, alienation, anger, heartbreak, she said.

Are there more? I said.

Maybe, she said.

Oh no, I said. And then, for some reason, I began to ramble on about languages, this torrential speech that had maybe been gestating inside of me for an unnaturally long time. I think Spanish is my favourite, I said. I told her that I had been born in Canada and started off speaking Plattdeutsch and then I went to school and learned English and loved it and never spoke Plattdeutsch if I could help it except with my dad who insisted on it. I told her that after school, if my dad was out, I'd teach my mom English words like *hula hoop* and *keep on trucking*. I told her I had a sister, Katie, and that we had whispered together all night long in English like other kids sneak smokes. I told her that when I was thirteen we moved to Mexico, to Chihuahua, and I started to learn Spanish even though my father had disapproved of that too.

Why? said Noehmi.

Girls weren't supposed to, I said.

Why? said Noehmi.

I don't know, I said. The usual reasons.

And then I told her that I was married to a Mexican guy and she said you are not!

I am, I said. But he left me.

And that's why you came to Mexico City? she said.

Sort of, I said. Noehmi looked closely at Ximena.

She doesn't look very Mexican, she said. But I guess she took after you. Do you share custody with your husband?

No, I said.

He doesn't want to see his kid? she said.

Well . . . actually, I said, Ximena isn't his kid.

Ahhh, said Noehmi. She smiled. She nodded her head as the universe revealed itself.

No, it's not that, I said. She's not my kid, either. She's my sister.

Really? said Noehmi. Why do you have her?

I don't know, I said.

Did your parents die? said Noehmi.

No, I said. I was beginning to understand something I couldn't articulate. It was a jazzy feeling in my chest, a fluttering, a kind of buzzing in my brain. Warmth. Life. The circulation of blood. Sanguinity. I don't know. I understood the enormous risk of telling the truth, how the telling could result in every level of hell reigning down on you, your skin scorched to the bone and then bone to ash and then nothing but a lingering odour of shame and decomposition, but now I was also beginning to understand the new and alien feeling of taking the risk and having the person on the other end of the telling, the listener, say:

Bad shit at home? You guys are running away?

Yeah, I said.

I understand, said Noehmi.

I wandered around the Zócalo looking for Aggie. I was a little nervous and also a bit relieved about the three of us being separated for the first time since our exodus. My arms were sore from holding Ximena and carrying stuff and I tried to drop my shoulders and shake out my stiffness and appear somewhat confident. I scanned the crowd but no Aggie. I headed towards the National Palace. It took me quite a long time to get to it because I had to meander around clumps of people and food stands and dancers and noisemakers and kids playing and mothers nursing babies and teenagers smoking cigarettes and old men and dogs and laughing families and praying nuns and choirs and pigeons and tarps and giant banners and unicycles and gladiators and boxers and soccer players. I saw a guy who looked exactly like Jorge and I stopped dead in my tracks, as they say, and panicked a little. It wasn't him and I didn't know if that made me feel happy or sad. Eventually it started to rain, gently at first and then hard. It felt good. People took out pieces of cardboard and garbage bags to protect themselves. I finally made it to the National Palace and went inside and there was Aggie staring at a massive mural. She was crying. I walked over to her and put my arm around her shoulders.

What's wrong, Aggie? I whispered.

She shook her head.

Are you afraid? I said.

No, she said.

I didn't know what to say or how to make her stop crying. I hugged her. I had forgotten how skinny she was.

Look at that, said Aggie.

The picture? I said.

It's called *México a través de los siglos,* she said.

It's making you sad? I said.

No, she said. Her face was covered in snot and she spoke in the spaces between her sobs.

I didn't know that a grown-up could do that, she said. She pointed at the mural. I didn't know that a person could do that.

I stared at it with her. She was in some kind of trance. Finally she asked me where Ximena was and I told her about Noehmi and that we should probably get back to her. If I had known more about anything I might have pointed out how Diego Rivera was asking all Mexicans to look squarely at the history of their lives, at the beauty and the misery and the pain and the struggle and the wreckage created by that profligate Cortés. I could have added too that Diego Rivera was completing his mural around the time the seven Mennonite men came to the palace to ask for the land in Chihuahua, now the scabby homeland of Aggie, Ximena and Pancho Villa, and how Mennonites always choose to live in places nobody else wants to.

Can we come back? said Aggie.

Of course! I said. As often as you like.

We snaked our way through the crowd and found Noehmi huddled under a lean-to made of garbage bags and using a flashlight to read her book . . . *And Other Problems in Waking Life.* Ximena was fast asleep under Noehmi's baggy sweater. Noehmi rested her chin on Ximena's head while she read.

There were fireworks going off in the rain. People were banging on pots again and there was sporadic shouting coming from all over the square. We crawled under the lean-to and sat down next to Noehmi and Ximena.

How was she? I said.

Perfection, said Noehmi.

Did she cry a lot? I said.

No, said Noehmi, hardly at all. I sang Jonathan Richman songs to her.

Who's that? said Aggie.

My hero, said Noehmi. He's old, like sixty or something, and he still loves the world and when you listen to his music he makes you love it too.

A guy walked past and said something about a blow job to Noehmi.

Go fuck yourself with Hitler's dick, said Noehmi happily. Are you guys hungry?

Noehmi's friends weren't there at that moment but they had cooked up some kind of meat with onions and peppers on a small barbecue they'd brought with them to the square. There are tortillas in that basket over there, she said.

While Aggie and I ate, Noehmi sang Jonathan Richman songs to all of us. We chewed and smiled and Aggie clapped.

Where did your friends go? said Aggie.

To get a camera, said Noehmi. They want to make a documentary about the protest.

Where are they going to get a camera? I asked.

I don't know, said Noehmi. They'll probably get sidetracked along the way. Or they'll come back with paint instead, or beer, or some new idea for a circus or something. They're social anarchists.

Oh, I said. I looked away. I scratched my arm and racked my brain for a fluid response and then quickly prepared some food.

Aggie and Noehmi were sleeping with Ximena between them on the tarp beside me. I tore a strip of material off my old dress and tied one end of it to Ximena's tiny wrist and the other end to Aggie's. When I lie down, I thought, I'll tie another strip of the dress from my wrist to Ximena's other wrist. And maybe one to Noehmi. I hope I don't wake her up. For a few seconds I thought about my little brothers who loved connecting things with rope. I wondered if I'd ever see them again and a torpedo of sadness struck me and moved straight through my body. Steady on, I said to myself. Earlier, right after the blow job incident, a man offered to buy Ximena, and Aggie pulled a knife on him, the new one that we bought earlier in the day. Noehmi's friends were called Alexis, Guillen, Dupont and Ernie. They're wasted, Noehmi told me. They were very nice and would die for her if she asked them to.

What do you mean wasted? I asked her. She said they were on another plane. She read something out loud to me from her book: *Katherine compared the energy of trauma to a cobalt bomb with a radioactive half-life of one hundred years.* I asked her what that meant and she said she didn't know exactly but that she loved the way it sounded. She thought maybe it meant that every trauma presents a choice: paralysis or the psychic energy to move forward.

Hmmm, perhaps, said Aggie, stroking her chin. I told her in Low German not to make fun of people who were more enlightened than her. She told me she was bored with shitball trauma talk and wanted to see more pictures. I told her to go to sleep and dream some up and she told me those were only words. But she did go to sleep, finally, thank God. After that Noehmi told me about her life. She told me that one year ago she broke up with her boyfriend and life became a nightmare. Her boyfriend was heart-broken. He tried to prevent her from leaving the apartment they shared and he drank non-stop all day and night. When she finally left to go and stay with her sister he somehow hacked into her emails. He suspected that she was seeing someone else and he tried to kill himself with booze and pills. All that stuff, she said. That crazy stuff. But it was desperate behaviour, she said. He had lost something he loved. There's no dignity in that. How can there be? He was a wild animal, she said. She told me that she still loved him.

Where is he now? I asked her. She pointed at Guillen and said right there. He's not my boyfriend anymore, she said. Dupont is. But Guillen has a different girlfriend. She said they were all friends. It was madness. It was awful. But that's normal. And now it's better.

I'm not sure what Noehmi's friends came back with, no camera anyway, none that I'd seen, but they were outside the lean-to singing now and playing drums in a circle. Other protesters were dancing around to their music and the rain had stopped and the air smelled clean. My desert friends, the stars, were invisible above the bright lights of the city.

In the middle of the night I untied myself from Aggie and Ximena and got up to find a pay phone. My fists were clenched when I woke up, ready to milk cows or kill kidnappers. Aggie was moaning in her sleep again like she was haunted. Dupont was sleeping next to Noehmi with his arm around her waist and the other boys were gone. The drums were piled neatly in a corner underneath the tarp. I had never used a pay phone before and I only knew one person with a phone. I put my coin in the slot and it fell into a little tray at the bottom. I did this over and over, like an idiot. An old woman walking past noticed that I was having trouble and helped me out. I thanked her and she held my face in her hands and squeezed. I tried to smile and she kissed me on both cheeks. I dialed Jorge's number and a man answered but it wasn't Jorge so I hung up. I didn't know what I would say to him anyway. I checked to see if my coin would come back to me. No. Well, I thought, now I know how a pay phone works. I didn't want to let go of the phone right away. I held it to my ear and pretended to have a conversation. I wondered if I was going crazy.

A guy with tattoos all over his body came and stood beside me, staring at the ground, waiting. I told my imaginary husband that I loved him and said goodbye. The man waiting for the phone had the name Esther tattooed across his throat.

It's all yours, I said, and he said thanks, I didn't mean to rush you. I started to walk away and the man said excuse me, but are you Irma Voth? My heart leapt into my throat and I whirled around to face him. How could this dark stranger possibly know my name?

That didn't happen.

I started to walk away and the man said excuse me, you forgot your bag.

Thanks, I said. I took the tattered *farmacia* bag from him.

Are you here alone? he said.

Yes, I said. Well, no, not alone.

You are or you aren't? said the man.

I'm not, I said.

That's good, he said, because it's dangerous for a woman to be on her own in Mexico City. Especially a tourist like yourself.

I'm not a tourist, I said.

You're from here? he said.

North of here, I said. But in Mexico.

I once lived just north of the border, he said. In El Paso.

I nodded and told him I'd been to El Paso a bunch of times.

I lived there with this woman, he said. He pointed to his throat.

Esther, I said.

Yes, he said. Esther. She's in Houston now.

He told me that he and Esther had managed to cross the border into Texas by paying off a guard and that they had made their way to El Paso where they both got jobs in a restaurant working under the table. Esther started to like one of the cooks and eventually she ran off with him and married him and even had a kid with him. The tattooed guy parked his car in front of Esther's new house and spied on her. He cried in his car and tried to get her to love him again by leaving gifts outside her door. Finally the guy she had married got fed up and called the immigration people and told them that this guy, the tattooed guy, was in America illegally and they kicked him out of the country, back to Mexico.

Now you're stuck with the tattoo, I said.

Yeah, he said, at first I wanted to have it removed but that costs a lot of money. I tried to turn it into a different word but I couldn't think of one.

In English you could have it say Rest Here, I said.

It's okay, he said. Now I'm happy to see the name Esther on my throat every day.

Because you have good memories? I said.

No, he said, because it reminds me of this treacherous world. If I'm ever foolish enough again to trust a woman I'll look at myself in the mirror and see her name and I won't make another mistake.

But it'll be backwards when you look in the mirror, I said.

It doesn't matter what it is, he said. I see the ink, I feel the pain of the needle pricking my throat, I see tiny bubbles of blood, and I'm reminded of the day I pledged my love to her.

There you go, I said. I'm Irma Voth. Pleased to meet you.

I'm Jeronimo Galvez Paz, he said. Likewise.

We shook hands and said goodbye.

When I got back to the tarp Aggie and Ximena were gone. I woke up Noehmi and Dupont and asked them if they knew where my sisters were and they said no, they hadn't noticed them leave. I stood next to Noehmi and Dupont, who were rubbing their eyes and clearing their throats, and looked in every direction for as far as I could see. It was dark so I saw very little.

We'll help you find them, said Noehmi. She told Dupont to get up and find his flashlight.

Do you have a flashlight? I asked him.

No, said Dupont. She always expects little miracles of me.

Let's go, man, said Noehmi. Why is this ribbon tied around my wrist?

But then she forgets about them, he said.

Noehmi and Dupont walked off in one direction, it might have been east, and I went north, or maybe south. The point is we split up and began our search. I could tell you all the things I was feeling but there is one picture that sums it up and that's the one of that skinny guy running across a bridge holding his face and being chased by a mushroom cloud. My sister Katie had that picture tacked to her bedroom wall and she liked to make word bubbles for the skinny man that had to do with reasons for his panic. One day she ripped it off her wall and stuffed it into her garbage can. She said it was ubiquitous.

It's really true that a person can become rigid with fear. I felt my limbs stiffen as I walked across the Zócalo calling out Aggie's name and imagining one horror after another, each scenario worse than the one before it. I prayed. I made a deal with God, wondering how I could have prevented all of this from happening, and hating myself. I punched myself in the side of my head. Think, Irma, I said. I stopped walking and stood still in the centre of the Zócalo and all of the protesters, sleeping and awake. I scanned the crowd, looking for one white-blond head that would pop out of the darkness like a piece of toast. Okay, I said to myself, how can this even be happening? How can I have lost all of my sisters? This is without a doubt the shittiest moment in the history of my life. Then the words *history of my life* started to carve some kind of repetitive groove in my brain. I touched the space between my eyes, the source of light, my internal . . . whatever. What had Marijke told me? The history of my life, I said. The source of my internal . . . light. This was stupid. And then I knew.

I ran towards the National Palace at the far end of the Zócalo and found Aggie leaning against the door, asleep, with Ximena in her arms. I woke her up and hugged them both. Aggie hugged me back. We stayed that way for a long time. And then I asked her when the doors opened and Aggie said she didn't know but if we waited there we'd be the first ones in when they did open.

I didn't know where you were, said Aggie. I woke up and you were gone. I freaked out.

I'm sorry, I said.

Where did you go? she said.

I went to find a phone, I said.

Why? said Aggie. Who would you call?

I didn't call anybody, I said.

Here, said Aggie, can you hold her? My arms are killing me.

I took Ximena and stuffed her inside my sweatshirt. I rubbed her back a bit and hoped she wouldn't wake up for a while. I needed to sleep.

A couple of hours later the doors to the National Palace opened up and Aggie went inside so that she could stare at her mural. I had managed to find Noehmi and Dupont in the meantime to tell them they could stop looking and we had agreed to have breakfast together on the tarp when Aggie was finished looking at art. I waited outside with Ximena and gave her a bottle. We sat in the sunshine and she looked at me while she drank and I scanned the crowds and looked at her every once in a while too and smiled and told her she was holding up well. Are you a little lamb? I asked her. I tried to shield her eyes from the sun. Are you a warrior? I said. I told her I'd find us a real home that day. Somewhere, you know, out there. In the city. This one. It feels good to make plans with a baby. They seem a little more flexible than the plans we make with people who remember making them.

We all ate a delicious breakfast of eggs and peppers and avocados together in the sunshine on the tarp. Another day of protest had arrived, we had survived the night, and it was time for the three of us to get organized.

Where do you want to go? said Noehmi.

I don't know exactly, I said.

What kind of job would you like to have?

I'm not sure, I said. Anything, I guess.

Do you have enough money for one month's rent? said Noehmi.

I'm not sure, I said. We ate our eggs and I silently critiqued my organizational skills. There were lists that I needed to make.

Do you have a job? I asked Noehmi.

We're students, said Noehmi. Most of us still live with our parents.

What are you students of? I said.

Art, said Noehmi. Politics. History. Cinematography. Dupont is studying madness in film.

Me and Irma work in the movie industry, said Aggie.

We do not *work* in the movie industry, I said. We helped out on one movie in Chihuahua.

What movie? said Dupont.

I think it's going to be called *Campo Siete*, I said.

Who's making it? said Dupont.

Diego Nolasco, I said.

Dupont stopped chewing and looked at me. Really? he said.

Yeah, I said. Do you know him?

Are you serious? said Dupont. You were working for Diego Nolasco?

Yeah, I said. Just as a translator.

I helped carry things, said Aggie.

After that Dupont talked for a long time about Diego's other movies and Aggie and I explained how it was that we had worked for him and Dupont found it all kind of hard to believe but I think we finally convinced him that it was true. Dupont said he sort of knew someone from his university who almost got a job working for Diego and I asked him if that person's name was Wilson and he said no, it was Roberto. He wanted to know if we were still in touch with Diego and I said no, it had ended a bit awkwardly. He's a genius, said Dupont. Yes, I said. Noehmi gave us the address of her sister's husband's brother who owns a bed and breakfast in Condesa, a different part of Mexico City with a huge park in the centre of it. You could ask him for a job, she said. She said she'd call him and ask him too. You'd be perfect because you can speak English to the tourists and you'd probably be able to carry Ximena around with you while you clean rooms or whatever.

We'll come and visit you, said Noehmi. She gave me another piece of paper with her phone number and address. She lived in a place called Tacubaya, not far from Condesa. She had drawn a picture next to her address for Aggie. It was of the National Palace with me, Ximena and herself standing in front of it. Where's Aggie? she had written in a word bubble coming from my mouth. In there! she had written in another word bubble coming from her mouth.

She said she wanted me to have her copy of *. . . And Other Problems in Waking Life*. But you haven't finished reading it yet, I said. She said I could read it in the meantime and she'd start reading another book called *The Outsider*, which was written by a Frenchman named Albert Camus. He died in a car crash, she said. And the novel he was working on went flying all over the road.

Do you know *Nausea*? she asked me.

Well, I said.

Jean-Paul Sartre? she said.

No, I said.

He was married to Simone de Beauvoir? she said. I'll bet you've heard of her.

No, I said.

Well, said Noehmi, she was this really intense woman. She had a passionate affair with an American writer named Nelson Algren. He's one of my favourite writers. He was mostly a recluse and then one day he decided he should smarten up and celebrate something and he decided to have a party at his place but just before the guests were due to arrive he fell down dead in his house.

Oh no, I said.

It's perfect, she said. But that was long after he had an affair with Simone de Beauvoir. She had fun fooling around with him in America but then she went back to Sartre who treated her like shit. And yet, she said, somehow she managed to inspire women to be free. I was nodding. Isn't that ironic? she said.

Yes, I said. It really is.

One of my favourite books from when I was a young teenager is by Antoine de Saint-Exupéry, said Noehmi. It's called *Wind, Sand and Stars*. I'll get it for you, Aggie. It changed my perception of the world. Aggie and I thanked her and Dupont a million times for their friendship and they said we would meet again, soon, maybe after exams, but that we should call any time if we needed anything.

NINE

DIOS CON NOSOTROS? said Aggie.

Yeah, I said.

So what? she said.

Just that, I said. I don't want to fight about it.

We were sitting on a bench in the park in the centre of Condesa. Ximena was lying naked in the sunshine airing out. I had just given her a bottle and she was making little squeaking sounds. Lots of dogs were running around and there were some guys trying to teach them new things. They wanted the dogs to stand still and not run until they'd been given a signal but the dogs just ran whenever they felt like it. Some of the guys yelled at their dogs and smacked them and some of the guys were very patient and sighed discreetly.

I miss Oveja, said Aggie. We were waiting for Noehmi's sister's husband's brother to return to work from his lunch break. His name was Hubertus. We were tired and hungry, the usual problems of waking life. I gave Aggie some money and sent her off to buy some tacos and juice from a stand nearby. Different types of people walked past me and I stared at them and tried to hear what they were saying to each other. I heard one woman gently tease her boyfriend about his pants. They were too short. But honey, she said, I understand. You can't worry about the mathematical permutations of the ringing of the church bells *and* the length of your pants at the same time. It's true, said the guy, something had to give. Then she laughed and they disappeared like dreams. An English-speaking couple walked past me and all I heard was: the quote artistic community close quotes . . . I watched them fade into the distance also. I took out my notebook to write some of these things down. I didn't know what these fragments meant. I wanted to talk like them. I wanted to talk like other people. And then Aggie came back with the tacos and we ate together sitting on the bench with Ximena lying between us. Aggie passed me a taco and some of the stuff fell onto Ximena's bare stomach and she pursed her lips like she wanted to kiss someone but her eyes were panicky and Aggie quickly licked it off her stomach before it could burn her.

Good hustle, I said.

What? she said.

That's what my old volleyball coach in Canada used to say after a good dig.

What? said Aggie.

That's what my old volleyball coach in Canada used to say after a good dig.

What are you—

I said that's what my old volleyball coach in Canada used to say after a good dig!

Yeah, but—

Just never mind, I said.

We waited. We watched people and didn't speak. Little bugs landed on Ximena and I blew them away. Then I asked Aggie what she was thinking about. She didn't answer. I asked her again and she folded her arms across her chest and stared at something way off in the distance. Home? I said. She didn't speak. I bet you're missing that kid, Isaac, that boy with the blood disease. Didn't you tell me that if he cut himself he'd bleed to death? Ximena wriggled in the sunshine and Aggie kept her mouth shut. That's why you had a crush on him, right? I said. Because every little thing he did was like risking his life? I got a diaper out of the *farmacia* bag and put it on Ximena before she peed all over the bench. Aggie's eyes were closed. Isn't that what you said about him? Aggie?

Didn't he let you wear his MedicAlert bracelet for a couple of days?

Nothing, she said.

What's nothing? I said.

You asked me what I was thinking about, she said. Stop talking to me. We waited some more. I thought about ways to cheer her up. Finally I saw Hubertus walking up the sidewalk and jingling a set of keys. He unlocked the front gate of the bed and breakfast. I told Aggie to watch Ximena and stay exactly where she was.

Seriously, Aggie, please, I said. I understand that your opinion of my words is that they are just words, and in so many ways but not in every way you are absolutely correct. I understand precisely how you would enjoy wielding your power in this situation by saying fuck that, fuck Irma and her bossiness, fuck this obedient little sister business, fuck all these cheesy little rules and regulations and getting up and wandering off and making me crazy with worry but I'm begging you now, like I have before, and like I will again, to stay put, to stay out of trouble and to not get lost. Your safety means everything to me, Aggie. Nothing is as important to me as your safety. Nothing. Please. I love you more than anything in this world, Aggie, and I can't bear to lose you. I just can't. The world would end. My world would end. Aggie, I'm begging you.

My words aren't only words. They're pictures and tears and imperfect offerings of love and self-inflicted shots to my brain. Please? Will you steadfastly remain on this very bench and not sell Ximena or in any way jeopardize your safety or hers? Will you promise to pull your knife on anyone wishing to mess with you or purchase your sister? Yes or no.

Tiny movements at the corners of Aggie's mouth. She was an Olympian in self-control.

Aggie, I said. This is so important. I'm going now to find myself a job. This job, which I will find, will ensure that you and I have food to eat and a roof to protect us from the rain and the sun and walls to keep away bugs and kidnappers. If I don't go right now I'll miss my chance and all our hopes will die in the street and the rain will wash them into the gutter and then down into the sewer and then out into the ocean miles and miles and miles beneath the surface where there is not enough oxygen to spend any time retrieving them. They will be gone for—

Will you just go already? said Aggie. You could have had a job by now and already been paid like twice.

Okay, but will you? I said.

Will I what? she said.

Stay right here and don't move?

Maybe, said Aggie.

Aggie! I said. For—

Yes! she said. Irma. God. Go already. You're like Tante Greita.

Tante Greita was the name we'd given to our slowest cow, the one we loved the most but that needed to be smacked on the ass a lot.

Okay, but will you tie her to your body? I said.

Ximena? said Aggie.

Just in case you fall asleep or something, I said.

Aggie didn't say anything. She got my old dress out of the *farmacia* bag and draped it around her shoulders. Then she picked up Ximena and held her to her chest with one hand and expertly wrapped the two ends of the dress around Ximena with her other hand. I smiled and thanked her and she nodded once, very dignified. Ximena's head was up high, close to Aggie's, and they were both looking off towards the park. I walked off towards the bed and breakfast and turned around to look at them. From a distance they looked like a two-headed monster. I waved, not expecting Aggie to notice, but she waved back. She was watching me too and my heart was overwhelmed with love.

Irma Voth, I said.

And you've just moved to Mexico City? said Hubertus. We had already established that it was because of Noehmi that I was there asking him for a job. We were sitting at a wrought iron table in a little courtyard belonging to the bed and breakfast. White curtains billowed out of open windows all around us and it felt like we were on a tall ship. There were bunches of flowers everywhere, white lilies that appeared to be opening as we spoke, and a few small trees and a thick green hose that snaked around and almost tripped me. My first instinct was to slice it in half with a machete. There was a narrow cement staircase that led up to a room with a red door and a balcony. I wanted to live there, in that room. A woman in high heels walked around sweeping up petals and two older men spoke German to each other in a corner. One of them told the other that to his knowledge there was no word for kindness in the German language and the other man laughed loudly and banged his hand on the table.

Yes, I said. My sister and I are here to study.

Study what? said Hubertus.

Art, I said.

Art, said Hubertus. He nodded slowly and smiled. I heard my father whispering in my ear. Art is a lie, he said. I smiled nervously back at Hubertus and braced myself. I felt my mother moving her hand in a slow circle around my back the way the earth orbits the sun. Love is not selfish, she said. When life is a shit storm your best umbrella is art, said Hubertus. He laughed. I heard that in a movie or something, he said. I'm sorry.

That's pretty funny, I said. I tried to laugh.

Have you seen any good movies lately? he said.

I've never seen a movie, I said. But I worked on one recently.

Well, he said. Whatever. So you're interested in working here in La Condesa. Where do you live?

We don't have a place yet, I said.

And your school?

After I've found a job and an apartment I'll start to look for schools, I said.

Would you like a cup of coffee? said Hubertus. That's a start. First things first. He laughed again and apologized. He asked the woman in high heels if she would mind bringing us two cups of coffee and when she came back she put her arms around his head and kissed the top of it and said not at all, *cachondo*, cream and sugar? And Hubertus closed his eyes and said *sí, baby, eres muy simpática.* The woman's name was Natalie.

This is Irma, said Hubertus. She and her sister are here in Mexico City to study art.

Ah, said Natalie. Lovely! You've come to the right place. Will you be focusing on a particular medium?

Yes, I said. Things began to happen to me, then, involuntarily. My foot began to tap the ground and my throat made a crude noise.

Yes? said Natalie. Do you mind me asking what it is?

I was silent, waiting for the world to end. I smiled and looked at her and she smiled back at me, kindly, with pity or patience or amusement or disbelief that this cave woman had managed to teleport herself into the future straight into her and Hubertus' courtyard.

Well, she said. It's not an easy thing to articulate, is it? I understand.

Thanks, I said.

But I'm fascinated with artists, she said. I love reading about their lives. You know how they say that so many artists are melancholic?

I nodded, clueless, and sipped my coffee.

Apparently, said Natalie, the part of the brain that can obsess over dark things like death and pain and nothingness, which is depression more or less, is the same part of the brain that allows a person to obsess over the infinite challenges of art which produces something like stamina. I don't know. Or focus. The focus required to complete one long query. Am I making sense?

Hubertus started laughing again and questioned her use of the word *query*, suggesting that *project* might be a better one, and I said yes. Natalie started laughing then too, and told me not to take things so seriously. If I'm not making sense, she said, then I'm not making sense. So what?

We drank our coffee and talked a little bit more about practical things. Natalie came over and asked me if I knew what the trees were called. I said no. She told me they were jacarandas. She said that one March two years ago she was feeling suicidal. She had planned to step in front of a bus. Then she looked at the jacaranda tree and changed her mind.

You decided to hang yourself from it instead? I said.

No! said Natalie. It was the exquisite patience of the tree. She described the way the jacaranda tree waited and waited and waited, barren, ignored, unexceptional, until a certain day in spring when it would erupt joyfully and comically into life. Purple flowers everywhere! she said. Small children are lost every spring, hidden in the purple flowers, cars crash into cars because they can't see anything but purple flowers, people plunge fully dressed into ponds because the water is carpeted with purple flowers and invisible! If the tree could wait all year for a relatively brief moment of beauty, said Natalie, and continue to stay alive for centuries, then so could I.

You'll stay alive for centuries? I said.

I'll stay alive, said Natalie. I'm a pupil of the jacaranda tree. It has taught me that it's okay to lay low most of the time, to nest in the shadows . . . and then . . . explode!

Hubertus laughed and laughed. Shit goes DOWN! he said. Natalie smacked him on the head and then she picked up the green garden hose and wrapped it around his neck while she kissed him and he pretended to die.

At the end of this encounter I had a job as a maid. I hadn't managed to work the existence of Ximena into the equation.

I didn't want to ruin my chance at employment by insisting that while on the job I carry a misanthropic infant around on my back. Maybe she could appear on the scene like a jacaranda tree, out of nowhere, and she would inspire Natalie to live.

I walked out onto the street and heard the whistles of the knife sharpeners and the cries of gas and water men. I wondered if in Mexico City it worked the other way around too so that I could walk up and down the streets shouting out the names of things I needed as opposed to the names of things I had for sale.

Aggie and Ximena weren't on the bench. At first I thought maybe I had gone to the wrong bench but I saw taco filling all over it and little bugs eating it so I knew it was the right one. I wondered why it happened so often in life that just as you secured one corner of the tent another one would flap loose in the wind. I stared at the little bugs and tried to think. A one-man trumpet, tambourine and drum band walked past me. I know, I thought, we have to do everything ourselves if we want it to get done. I told myself to inhabit the mind and body of Aggie. I'm Aggie, I said. I'm sitting on the bench bored to death, restless as hell and poised to bolt. Where do I go? I saw a large statue, a sculpture of a woman, and I walked towards it. It was a buxom nude holding two jugs of spouting water. I stood next to her and looked around for Aggie and Ximena. In Chihuahua I couldn't shake Aggie and in Mexico City I couldn't keep her from taking off. I kept walking. A guy sat on the ground with books spread all around him. I stopped and stared at them.

Hay algún libro de Simone de Beauvoir? I said.

No, no tenemos, he said.

Me puede recomendar algún libro? I said.

Sí, he said. *Te gusta . . . ?*

No sé, I said.

Que tipo de libros lees? he said.

No sé, I said.

Has leído Nuestra arma es nuestra palabra*?*

I had bought my first book. *Our Word is Our Weapon.* Selected writings of Subcomandante Insurgente Marcos. Actually I hadn't paid for it because Aggie had the *farmacia* bag with Ximena's stuff and all our money but the guy sitting on the ground told me I could have it for nothing if I came back and bought something another time.

Will you? he said.

Yes, I said.

I remembered a similar conversation I'd had with Wilson when he told me that he was going to Mexico City to deliver the film reels and keep them safe from my father. I wondered what he said when he got back to Chihuahua and Diego told him that I had left. Maybe: Drat. Or maybe he hadn't said a word. Maybe he'd written a little story about me in his notebook that he would read someday at the festival in Guadalajara. I'd be there, somehow, in a wonderful outfit, standing in the darkness of the crowd, and I'd hear him speaking through the microphone. I wouldn't be able to see him because of very tall people in front of me but I'd hear my name and

I'd follow his impassioned voice towards him, towards the light.

I smiled at the bookseller. I held up my book and said thanks again and he saluted me and called me comrade. I found Aggie dancing by a pond. She was in a class of people learning how to tango. Ximena was tied to her chest and Aggie had never danced in her life so her movements were a little awkward but she was concentrating hard on keeping up with the instructor. The other students had partners but Aggie's was imaginary. She flung her head back and thrust her chest with Ximena on it out towards the water and strutted across the grass. Her arm shot up and then she brought the back of her hand down and swept it across her eyes tragically as if to erase all the horror and misery she'd seen.

Excellent! Excellent! the instructor said.

The music stopped and Aggie looked around and grinned at a few of her fellow students. The class was over. I walked up to her and said hello and she said oh, sorry, you're done already? I was just on my way back to the bench. Did you get a job?

Yeah, I said. I'm a maid.

I'm a dancer, she said. She stuck her elbows out and snapped her fingers.

Well, I said. I get paid.

Well, she said. I get applause.

Well, I said. I get paid and with that money I rent an apartment and buy food. And a television.

Well, she said. I get applause and with that affirmation of my amazing talent I feel happy and confident and cool.

Well, I said. Enjoy your life as a dancer.

Well, she said. Enjoy your life as a maid.

Thanks, I will, I said.

Good, she said.

We walked in grim silence towards something else. Ximena was squirming and gurgling with joy. She loved a good fight. I didn't know where we were going. When Aggie asked me if I could hold Ximena for a while I asked her if she could stay on one fucking bench for a while.

That's very mature, she said. I walked ahead of her and didn't look back for ages but when I did she was still there, tagging along. I asked her to put my book into the *farmacia* bag and then I noticed that she didn't have it.

Aggie! I said. Where's the bag?

We ran back to the pond and looked around but it was gone. No big surprise. We gazed out at the water and stared at our murky reflections. What would Gustavo Mundo, the taxi driver from Acapulco, think about all this? That losing all our money and material belongings was worth learning how to dance the tango? I guess that made as much sense as anything.

Well, said Aggie. So we have a book now.

Yeah, I said. I held it up like a papery shield.

We're doomed, she said.

I'm sorry.

Sure, I said.

When do you start your job?

Tomorrow morning.

I'm really, really sorry.

I am.

I am!

Show me some of your moves, I said.

Aggie looked a little shy. She untied Ximena from her chest and laid her out in the grass. X. immediately sprang into mortal combat with invisible enemies.

I could teach you, said Aggie.

Aggie and I badly danced the tango in the dying light while Ximena punched away the ghosts.

That night we tried to sleep in the park, leaning up against a statue of a handsome man that we pretended was our father, but the police told us we couldn't do that. We had no food for Ximena. The only way we could stop Ximena from screaming with hunger was to walk around so that's what we did. All around avenidas Michoacán, México and Amsterdam. Avenida Amsterdam had originally been a racetrack that circled the park. We walked a million laps. We kept watch over each other while we peed in bushes. We activated some kind of alarm on a blue car when we leaned against its bumper. We ran. We were cold. Aggie cried a little bit and said again how sorry she was. I tried to comfort her. We made up rhymes in Low German and tried to remember jokes. When we passed under street lamps we read a little bit of Subcomandante Insurgente Marcos's selected writings. We accepted a few pesos from a happy drunk couple who called us curious and wondered if we were real or a mirage. Sometimes we'd sit down on the grass but then Ximena would start to scream and I was afraid the police would get mad. In the early morning, when the sun began to rise, we gave our pesos to a fruit vendor setting up his cart and he gave us some avocados and juice in a plastic Baggie. Aggie peeled the avocados with her knife and we dipped them in the juice and tried to get Ximena to suck on them. I asked the vendor if he had an old rag I could use as a fresh diaper for Ximena and he gave me a soft white cloth with a picture of the Empire State Building on it. We washed our faces in a public fountain. I knew I would have to ask Hubertus for an advance on my wages and that made me nervous.

At 7:30 a.m. or maybe 8:00 the three of us stood on the sidewalk in front of the bed and breakfast.

Pray now, I told Aggie.

For what? she said.

What do you think? I said. Everything.

I don't know where to begin, said Aggie.

And let me do the talking, I said.

The real talking? said Aggie.

Yeah, I said. You pray silently for mercy while I speak out loud to Hubertus.

How will we keep Ximena from screaming? she said.

That's part of the prayer for everything, I said.

We could wait in the park, said Aggie.

No, I said. We tried that and you went dancing. Just put some avocado on your finger and put it in her mouth.

We could just walk around the block while you're talking to what's his name, said Aggie.

Forget it, I said. Pray.

TEN

WE WERE ALL SITTING IN THE little courtyard drinking hot coffee and eating eggs and beans and oranges. Natalie had run out to buy formula and a plastic bottle and some diapers for Ximena from the little store across the street. Aggie tried to drink from the green garden hose and I whispered to her in Low German that she shouldn't. Hubertus pretended not to have noticed and quickly brought us a bottle of water and some pineapple juice.

Aggie thanked him in Spanish and told him she'd been dying of thirst. She poured some of the water out of the glass bottle into her hand and splashed it on her face.

Aggie, I whispered. It's just for drinking.

You are sisters and you are Mexicans? he said.

Yes, I said.

What language are you speaking?

Spanish, I said.

I know, he said, but to each other.

Low German, I said.

I've never heard of Low German, said Hubertus. Is it like regular German?

Yeah, sort of, I said. Natalie had returned with the baby stuff and was preparing the bottle in the little kitchen next to the courtyard.

Irma, he said, I don't want to make you uncomfortable but there are some questions I have to ask.

All three of us stared at him and he laughed.

Don't be afraid, he said. You should see your eyes. All six of them! You girls are funny.

Sorry, I said.

Sorry for what? said Hubertus. He laughed again. I could tell that he was a little spooked by Aggie's wolf eyes, or maybe he wasn't. But she could go for ages without blinking like she was challenging you to fill the empty whites of her eyes up with something better than what she was seeing right then. She could wait forever.

Okay, he said. I have to ask you. Why are your little sisters here with you? I'm so sorry if this is a difficult question to answer. Is it?

Yes, I said. I tried to put the pieces of my life together in my head before I blurted out a stupid answer. I wanted to tell the truth but the truth, in its plain dress, was so ugly. I didn't want to say those words in front of Aggie because I thought they'd make her feel lost and helpless all over again. If I were somebody else I could answer with a mural or a tango down by the pond in the park or a poem. If I were Wilson. Or a gun if I were my father.

I'm sorry, said Hubertus. But if your parents are looking for you, I need to know. Your sisters are only children, still.

Natalie came trotting out of the kitchen in her high heels holding the bottle up like a victory flag. Here! she said. Let me feed that poor baby. May I? I handed Ximena over to Natalie and whispered that I was sorry she was so filthy. Natalie waved that all away, nonsense she said, and held X. close to her chest while she fed her.

They're not, I said.

They're not children? said Hubertus.

They're not looking for us, I said.

The only sounds in the courtyard were birds and Ximena ferociously sucking. I thought she might devour the plastic bottle itself and live forever with its outline bulging in her stomach.

How can you be sure? said Hubertus. Are they dead? I'm sorry for asking.

No, I said. They're alive as far as I know. Hubertus smiled and nodded. Aggie took a sip of pineapple juice. I noticed a plane flying high in the sky and spelling out a word with its jet stream, but then it disappeared.

My father doesn't like us, I said. He doesn't like girls. He doesn't like it when we get older and . . . there's something about his daughters that makes him crazy and . . . that's all.

Natalie looked up from her job feeding Ximena, and Hubertus looked at her and then at Aggie who may or may not have blinked.

My God, said Natalie.

Natalie, he said.

What? she said. Am I not allowed to speak?

Does he know where you are? said Hubertus.

No, I said. Nobody does.

What about your mother? he said. Won't she want you to come back?

Not if he's there, I said.

Hubertus nodded and tried to look grim. He spread his fingers out and examined the backs of his hands. He made loud breathing sounds. Then he rubbed his thighs vigorously. He looked at Natalie who had gone back to feeding Ximena. She ignored him. The birds continued to sing, or to make noises anyway.

So, said Hubertus finally. And you lost all your money when Aggie here (he nodded at Aggie and smiled) decided to enrol in an impromptu tango class in the park?

Yes, I said. She put the bag down.

Well, said Aggie, you can't dance the tango with a *farmacia* bag.

But you can dance it with a baby? I said in Low German.

What was I supposed to do? she said.

You could've stayed on the bench and not danced at all, I said.

I wasn't going to—

You could have stayed out of trouble, I said in Spanish.

Well, said Hubertus, what's life without trouble?

Yeah, Irma, said Aggie. What's life without trouble?

Yeah, I know life isn't life without trouble, I said, that's pretty clear. I'm just saying that you don't have to be the one to cause it all the time. Why don't you give somebody else a chance every once in a while?

I'm not! said Aggie. You're the one who married a—

Aggie, I said. Shut up.

You're married? said Hubertus.

Yeah, I said, but I don't know where he is, my husband.

Does he know that you're here? said Hubertus.

No, I said.

Hubertus asked Natalie to join him in the office of the bed and breakfast where their computer and desk were. Are they fucking now? said Aggie when they were gone.

If you want to live in a big city, I said, you have to learn not to say the first thing that comes to your mind because there are actually people here who can hear it. There's a population here.

Yeah, but they're strange people, don't you think? she said.

When they came back they told us we could live in a little room that was a part of the bed and breakfast. It was upstairs and in the back, overlooking other rooftops. It had a big bed and a pullout couch and a bathroom and a sink and a little fridge and a microwave oven and some painted pictures of fruit and other things on the wall and a tiny balcony. I would make breakfast for the guests in the morning and clean rooms and run errands in the afternoon. Aggie would go to school. Ximena would hang around being taken care of by me or by Natalie or Hubertus. In the evening I'd teach Natalie English so that one day she could pursue her dream of reading the complete works of Charles Dickens in their original form. Or something like that. She and Hubertus were laughing their heads off when they said it.

I don't know how to thank you, I said. I'll never forget your kindness.

Let's go, said Natalie. I'll show you your room and you can get some sleep and when you wake up we'll have lunch.

I don't know how to thank you? said Aggie in Low German. That's a stupid thing to say. We were lying in the giant bed with Ximena clean and fresh-smelling and drunk with satisfaction between us. You say thank you, said Aggie. Like this. Thank you.

I wish I was as smart as you, Aggie, I said.

I know, me too, she said. I pray for that every night.

Thanks, I said.

I've almost given up, though, she said.

Yeah, I understand, but thanks anyway, I said. Not only are you exceptionally smart you're also kind-hearted and considerate.

She moved her shoulder over a few inches so that it touched mine and then she moved back.

Are you being affectionate? I asked her.

When we woke up, Ximena had soaked the bed, right through her diaper and sleeper, through the blanket and the top sheet and the mattress protector and the mattress.

Shit, this kid is a lot of work, said Aggie.

We rinsed all that stuff in the shower and hung it over the balcony railing to dry. It was getting dark again. We went downstairs to find Hubertus and Natalie but they weren't around. There was a note for us. It was written on the back of an envelope and taped to the door of the office. They would be back late and there was some cash in the envelope that we could use to buy some food and diapers and there was also a small key to the kitchen, where the washer and dryer were. I'd start work in the morning. We went into the kitchen and ate some tortillas and cheese and salad. Then we wandered off into the neighbourhood to find a place where we could get our hair cut. We would use some of the food money. We wanted what we referred to as pixie cuts. Jagged and short. It was the only style I could remember from when I lived in Canada. Katie got one before she left for Vancouver, before she *tried* to leave for Vancouver, and it was maybe the first step on the road to our father's madness. I remember her showing it to me in our room and her whispering to me that it was called a pixie cut and this'll make him blind with rage and me agreeing and experiencing intense pain in my chest and stomach while she pranced around admiring herself, smiling at her reflection, fearless.

While we were getting our hair cut in a small shop on Avenida Michoacán the power went out and we were in the dark. The hairdresser asked us to wait for a few minutes but the power didn't come back on and Ximena was getting restless in my lap and banging her head against my collarbone and I was pulling bits of my hair out of her mouth and off her face and so we decided to pay and leave. The hairdresser asked us to come back the next day so that she could finish cutting our hair. When we got outside we saw each other in the light of the street lamp and Aggie laughed so hard she said she thought she'd wet her pants and I told her to try not to because she only had one pair.

You look like Wilf! she said. Wilf was my younger cousin, the one who lived in the filmmakers' house before he and his family went back to Canada. Three men walked past us and called us ugly *gringas* and Aggie swore at them in the coarsest Spanish slang I had ever heard. Not even from Jorge. Or Diego. We went back to the bed and breakfast and went into the kitchen and found a pair of scissors and took them back to our room. We brought a chair onto the balcony and Aggie finished cutting my hair. I picked up the blond strands and felt their baby softness between my fingers and then I threw them into the garbage can. I put my feet up on the railing. I offered to finish cutting her hair too but she said she liked the asymmetry of it and I shouldn't bother. Then we stared off at the city of Mexico, the D.F., the borough of Cuauhtémoc, our new home. We stayed out on the balcony for a long time looking at the lights and listening to the traffic and all the sirens. Way off in the distance we saw a building on fire. We talked a little bit about the things we had left behind, but not much. We talked about the universe, about loneliness. We talked about how to fall, the right way and the wrong way, to prevent injury, and if we could see our shadows from the light of Venus. We got a little cold but neither one of us wanted to go inside to get our sweatshirts because Ximena was dormant on the bed and we didn't want the sound to activate her.

That night Ximena woke up every hour on the hour howling at the world for all its timid resignation and coy duplicity and also, I think, at me directly for having no hair that she could twist around her little fist and pull until it came out by its roots. She could still vomit on me, though, so she did that a couple of times and then to top it off she head-butted me in the nose which actually brought tears to my eyes and made me plop her on the bed next to Aggie more roughly than I should have. Aggie woke up and said no, get her away from me and I said no, you have to walk around with her for a while now. I have to sleep.

I don't know what happened after that because Aggie took over and I lost consciousness. When I woke up they were both lying on the pullout couch, their eyes closed, their mouths wide open like sleep had caught them by surprise. If they'd been my captors this would be the moment I'd choose to run. A vile odour emanated from Ximena's ass. I peered closely at her chest and saw it rise and fall and rise again and thought: you live.

I went into the tiny bathroom and looked at myself in the mirror. Short and jagged. Good. I stroked the naked nape of my neck. I lifted up one lock of hair near my ear and measured it. One, maybe one and a half inches. Good. I looked at myself some more. Did I look like Katie? I don't know. I wanted to show my mother my new haircut. She would have smiled and shaken her head and kissed me. She would have been afraid for me. She would have covered her eyes and then peeked through them. She would have admired my daring. She would have rejoiced quietly, silently, and stored this moment in some dark and hidden pocket of her soul. I stared at myself a bit longer and tried so hard to see Katie. I tried to see my mother and I even tried to see my father.

The stuff that happened next was almost calm and manageable so I won't go into much detail. Aggie started school in September. She has a navy blue and white uniform that she hates and a clarinet that she practises on the balcony and one or two friends that come around every once in a while. She is drawing murals on our walls, on large sheets of wrapping paper that Hubertus buys in bulk. She has a so-called boyfriend whose name is Israel and who is also, coincidentally, a hemophiliac, so they must be careful when they punch each other and play around or he'll bleed to death. That's her type. The kind of kid who understands a soft and wounded interior. Israel told her that even sharp words can injure him but that was just a joke. His latest plan is to become a chainsaw artist. I've seen Israel run up the side of a building and then do a backwards somersault and land on his feet. He says that's his calling card.

I'm working. Cleaning rooms, making meals. Ximena, my antagonist, sits in her baby chair and watches me. Aggie and I both have cellphones. I tried to phone Jorge again and the operator told me that number was no longer in service. Otherwise I have Aggie's number and Hubertus's and Natalie's numbers and also Noehmi's number. We go for beers sometimes when she's not too busy with university classes and anarchy. Sometimes I walk over to the park to spy on that bookseller. I think and wonder a lot about Jorge. I wonder if he ever thinks about me or if he misses me at all. I wish I had been a better wife. And sometimes I pretend that I see Wilson. In bed, before I get up to work, I lie in the dark and imagine conversations with him and I remember the way he moved his hand across my body.

Ximena has learned how to bite and sit and point and lure people with her good looks. The tourists here at the bed and breakfast love her at first and then she starts to fight with them, stiffening her body into a blunt weapon, grabbing their noses and cheeks and lips and ears and twisting, screaming like an injured bird, and they give her back to me. Natalie says that when Ximena learns to walk Mexico City will know destruction similar to the scale of the 1985 earthquake.

Aggie's murals are almost all of our family. But they're conceptual, she says. Katie is a ghost that hovers over every scene and sometimes takes the shape of a crow or a breeze and Aggie is a rabbit. Our little brothers appear, when they appear, as raindrops. Our mother is a barn and I'm a tractor and our father is a big bell or the wreckage of the broken crop-duster. Aggie paints murals with these figures in different positions and doing different things. Sometimes she has us saying things, even the barn, but not usually. Aggie doesn't talk much about her murals and I've learned not to ask too many questions. One thing I like to ask and she doesn't seem to mind answering is: where's Katie in this one? I don't know if the purpose of each of her murals is to create a picture in which Katie can appear, or if she feels more free talking about the thing that represents Katie because she doesn't remember much about her so she isn't hampered by reality. One day I asked her where God was in her murals and she said TBA. I asked her what that meant and she said she didn't know but I'm pretty sure she does.

The other day I went out to buy some avocados and I took a different route to the store. I noticed a building with a sign on it that said *Citlaltépetl Refuge House.* There was a white poster in the window at the front of the building and there were black words on it that said, *When I came to Mexico City, I was dead. And here I started to live again.* There was a small open archway at the front of the building that led into a quiet courtyard. I walked inside and stood next to a wall with photographs on it. A woman came out of a little office and asked me if she could help me with anything and I told her I had seen the white poster in the window and it had made me curious about the building.

What happens here? I asked her.

We are a refuge for exiled writers, she said. The words on the poster are a quote from the Kosovar poet Xhevdet Bajraj.

Oh, I said.

Where are you from? she asked me.

From here, I said. I'm Mexican. I live a few blocks from here.

We have a few apartments for writers who are forced to leave their own countries, she said. And a small bookstore and library and a little café, as you can see. We have readings here sometimes and different types of events. Music, drama. We've tried to create a comforting and stimulating environment. She pointed at the tables set up in the courtyard.

Why are they forced to leave their own countries? I said.

For various reasons, said the woman. She explained some of those reasons to me and I nodded.

How do they leave? I said.

In different ways, she said. But always with unfinished business and a broken heart. Freedom has its price.

Where is he now? I said.

Who? she said.

The poet.

He lives nearby, she said. Here in La Condesa.

Well, I said. I didn't know what else to say. Then I thought of something. I have to go buy avocados, I said.

The woman said she understood. She loved them too. She thanked me for visiting and told me to keep one eye open for future events.

Last night Aggie agreed to guard Ximena, as she puts it, and I went out for a beer with Noehmi at a place called Tinto's which is sort of a halfway mark between her neighbourhood of Tacubaya and my neighbourhood of La Condesa. We sat across from each other in a red booth and she told me about the play she's working on.

It's a one-man show, she said. It takes place in total darkness until the very end. The audience hears voices and sounds but they don't see anything. She explained to me that at first the audience will hear the voice of a man, obviously suffering in some way. Then we'll hear the voice of a woman talking to a different man, then other voices, of kids, older people, a teacher. Gradually we'll realize that this man, the first man, is stuck in an air duct in the attic of a pawnshop that he's trying to rob so that he can buy drugs. It's his friend's pawnshop. The woman is his girlfriend and she's in the shop asking his friend if he's seen her boyfriend. He's been missing for days. His friend says he hasn't and starts flirting a bit with the woman. The man in the duct can hear all of this and it's killing him. But he's dying anyway. He's been there for a couple of days and he's dying of thirst. We realize that the other voices are the voices of the people he's remembering, the people in his life, his parents and his brother and his high school teacher. They are the voices of the people he is leaving behind as he dies. At the end of the play the lights come on for the first time and we see a man in a glass duct on the stage. That's all. There's no sound. No more voices. His face is pressed against the glass and he is dead. People don't know if it's over. They don't know if they should leave. Then, eventually, everyone does leave. They figure out that the play is over.

What do you think? said Noehmi. Do you think it'll work?

Definitely, I said.

Dupont is making the duct right now at his mother's apartment.

I'd like to see it, I said.

Actually, said Noehmi, I was wondering if you would provide one of the voices. It would just be a recording. But obviously the voices are really important because there's nothing else. I have to get them right.

I'd be one of the man's memories? I said.

Yeah, said Noehmi. I think your voice would be good for his second grade teacher. When he remembers her telling him that he can accomplish anything in life if he works hard and wants it badly enough.

I don't speak Spanish very well, I said.

Yeah you do, said Noehmi. You have an interesting accent and that's why your voice will be cool in the play. It'll stand out a bit from the others so that when your voice is heard the audience will be able to differentiate it more easily from the other female voices. You know what I mean?

I guess, I said.

He really likes her sandals and wants to marry her, said Noehmi. They're white and red and have three straps on them that cross the foot and a wedge heel. He starts putting on a bolo tie when he goes to school and slicking his hair over to one side to impress her.

The teacher?

Yeah, said Noehmi. And once, in the hallway after recess, he asks her to dance and that makes her laugh.

Does she dance with him? I asked. I thought about Jorge trying to teach me that dance, how I had failed him so spectacularly.

Well, I'm not sure if that will be explained, said Noehmi.

I'd say no, she doesn't, so he dances alone in the hallway. But he doesn't mind because he knows that he's impressed her and made her laugh.

Ah, I said. I smiled. For some reason, I don't know which one, I remembered my missionary aunt explaining to me in great detail how the jungle tribes of Ecuador used hot rocks to shrink heads. The features of the shrunken face remained exactly the same as they had been normally, except they were much smaller.

So? said Noehmi. Will you do it?

Of course, I said.

The next day I went for a walk, late in the day, before dinner. I took X. with me because Aggie was busy being taught skateboard tricks by Israel and I didn't want to go through fathoms of grief asking her to babysit. I had an uneasy feeling in my gut. I was a little nervous. There's a word in Low German for the way I felt but translated it means on top of and below a runaway horse which . . . well, I don't really know how to describe what I was feeling. It was too complicated and I was too stupid to unravel it all.

I walked past the bookseller in the park. Then I walked past him again. And one more time until I worked up the nerve to stop and say hello. The bookseller asked me if we had met once before and I said yes and that he had given me a book which I hadn't paid for. I handed him some money and he said thank you and asked me if I wanted another book and I said yes, but now I had no more money.

Again! Credit, he said, to keep you coming back. He smiled at me and I looked at the trees. He asked me if Spanish was my mother tongue and I said no. He said then what is? English?

No, I said. German. He rummaged around in his pile of books and gave me a copy of a book called *Jakob von Gunten.* It was written by Robert Walser, in German, a long time ago, around the turn of the last century. The bookseller told me that he kept books in different languages for tourists who happened to wander past looking for something to read. Robert Walser liked to walk around a lot, he said. He lived in a mental asylum for twenty years and somebody asked him if he was there to write and he said no, I'm here to be mad, and then one day he went for a long walk and lay down under a tree and died, said the bookseller. That's all I know about him. I hope you like the book. I thanked him and said goodbye. Then he asked me what my name was and I said Irma Voth.

What's yours? And he said it was Pushkin. But that I could call him Asher.

I stared at my new book. I flipped it over and flipped it over. What's it about? he said. I think it's about a boy who goes to servant school, I said. And then at the end he and the principal walk off into the desert.

All right, said Asher. Is that your baby? he said. Yes and no, I said. She's my sister actually. Asher waved at Ximena who stared at him soulfully. Natalie had bought a stroller for her and sometimes when she was in it she became curiously reflective. Asher handed X. a cardboard baby book and she took it and put it in her mouth and gnawed at it with a terrible hunger. Then she flung it so that it barely missed Asher's head and it fell onto the ground. He picked it up and gave it back to her.

Ximena and I kept walking. I pushed the stroller down the sidewalk towards the house of refuge for exiled writers. There were posters on the windows advertising different types of classes available to the general public.

The Bubbling Phenomena and Non-Compactness.

The "Almost Nothing" Precariousness in Art Since the 60s.

Taming Complexity.

Did Homer Describe an Eclipse in the *Odyssey*?

I read these posters and said the words out loud to Ximena. What do you think? I asked her. Did he or didn't he? She craned her head around and up to glare at me while I read. She had black rings of dirt around her neck. She wanted to keep moving.

When we got back home Aggie was alone and lying on the bed on her back. She told me she had something to show me and then she lifted her sweatshirt and showed me her belly button. There was jewellery stuck to it. I had it pierced, she said. Israel paid for it with his allowance. There was a tiny blue heart on a silver ring.

Does it hurt? I asked her.

Of course! she said. But I've got stuff to keep it clean.

Ximena had fallen asleep in her stroller so I left her there and lay down on the bed next to Aggie and closed my eyes. She asked me what was wrong and I said I didn't know. I was tired. I told her that I had used expensive perfume to kill some ants in a guest's room instead of going to the supply bin in the cellar to get the real bug killer because I didn't feel like going all that way. Then I panicked because the room smelled like perfume and I was sure that the guest would tell Hubertus or Natalie that I had used some of it for myself. So I lit a match to get rid of the perfume smell and then the room smelled like sulphur. I tried to turn the overhead fan on but the guest had hung wet clothing on it to dry and it was so heavy that the fan didn't spin very well and then stopped altogether and started to smell a bit like smoke. So then I opened the window to get rid of the sulphur smell and the smoke smell and the perfume smell but the screen was missing so a zillion flies flew into the room. Then I had to spend the next twenty minutes killing them and cleaning their bodies off the various surfaces and the whole time I was sweating like a horse because I was so afraid that the guest would come back to her room.

Did she? said Aggie.

No, I said.

What kind of perfume was it? she said. Poison?

Is that a kind? I said.

Yeah, said Aggie. Christian Dior.

What do you mean? I said.

Christian Dior is the name of the designer who makes the perfume, said Aggie.

How do you know that? I said.

Me and Israel get samples for his mom, she said.

I told Aggie that all the noise and confusion on the streets was overwhelming me a little bit. I told her that I missed the stars in Chihuahua and the sound of the wind rustling the corn.

Me encanta este lugar, said Aggie.

I know, I said. She was speaking mostly Spanish these days. She had told me that she liked it here.

I asked Aggie to tell me about her day in Plattdeutsch.

Why? she said. It was boring.

No, I mean just talk to me about anything in Plattdeutsch, I said.

She told me that she had gone to the museum of anthropology that day with her class and that she had really wanted to steal a tiny little artifact, a charm or something, that had once belonged to an Aztec warrior.

But you didn't, did you? I said.

Of course not, she said, you can't. They're under glass.

Oh, I said. But you wouldn't have anyway, would you? I said.

I don't know, she said. I might have if I thought I wouldn't be caught.

You would? I said.

Maybe, she said.

Don't, I said.

Why not? said Aggie.

Because it's stupid, I said. And you know it.

Then we started talking about Katie because I had remembered the time she'd been arrested for assaulting a police officer. She'd been walking home late from a bush party and the cop had stopped to ask her what she was doing out so late and she was kind of drunk and she kicked his car and told him it was none of his business so he drove along beside her saying stupid things and she was getting madder and madder and she threw her lip gloss at his face and so then he made the decision that it was his business after all and he stopped the car and dragged her into the back seat. She kicked and screamed and swore and that resulted in more assault charges or maybe mischief or something or other and she had to spend the night in jail.

She spent the night in jail? said Aggie.

Yeah, I said.

That's so fucking cool! said Aggie. Nobody ever tells me anything about Katie. What kind of lip gloss was it?

I don't know, I said. Chocolate mint.

What happened after that? said Aggie.

You don't want to know, I said.

I do so! said Aggie. You can't stop the story there. You don't know what I want to know and what I don't want to know.

Don't you know? I said.

No, she said. How would I know?

Well, I said. How do you think someone like Dad would have felt about his daughter being arrested for assaulting a police officer when she was coming home drunk from a bush party and then spending the night in jail?

All she did was throw lip gloss at him! said Aggie.

Aggie, I said.

What? she said.

You know exactly what, I said. You don't have to use your imagination.

After that Aggie did fun things to try to cheer me up. Sometimes she'd grab me around the waist when I wasn't expecting it, yell surprise and throw me down on the bed. I tried to do it to her one time and she laughed but said that I had to be careful with her belly button. She made up a game she called Baby Detective. I'd be lying in bed reading my new book or sitting on the balcony tying my shoes to get ready for work and I'd feel something. I'd sense that somebody was watching me. And I'd turn to see Ximena's big, spooky eyes. Sometimes from low down, close to the floor, and sometimes from high up, near the ceiling. Aggie would stand behind the open door and hold Ximena in different places so that only her spying little baby face poked out.

Then one afternoon when I was finished cleaning I went into our room to have a short nap. Ximena was in a playpen in the courtyard and Natalie was keeping an eye on her while she fixed up the planters. It was a very bright day and I had opened all our curtains in the morning when I went to work so that the sun would wake Aggie up for school. But when I walked into our room the curtains were closed and it was completely dark. Much darker than usual. I couldn't see anything. And there was a strange noise. I whispered Aggie's name and waited. I stood perfectly still for a minute trying to understand what was going on. Slowly, as my eyes adjusted to the darkness, I began to see little dots of silver light. At first I saw only a few but as time passed the room was filled with them and soon I was surrounded by them. I smiled. I understood. Aggie had covered the windows with thick, dark material she had found somewhere, maybe it was painted cardboard from school, and had used a pin or something tiny to prick hundreds of holes into the blackness to create sunlit stars. I took a step into the darkness and bumped into something hard. It was a floor fan, a small one, that Aggie must have tied strips of newspaper to and the fan was blowing them to make a noise like wind. I backed up a bit and felt the wall. It was cool and smooth. I carefully sat down on the floor and leaned against the door. I sat in the dark. I stared at the stars and listened to the wind.

I was still sitting there when Aggie came home from school and barged through the door and knocked me over. She switched on the lights and then said oh, you're here! There was a gecko on the wall beside my head. Aggie put her face next to it and said hey there, little gecko boy, did you enjoy your trip to Chihuahua? I thanked her for her gift of wind and stars and she said yeah, no problem, it was easy and then she showed me a giant painting she'd done in art class. It was of Katie in jail, doing a karate kick in her cell, her braids flying straight out behind her, trying to kick out the walls.

It's called *Chocolate Mint Lip Gloss*, said Aggie.

Wow, I said.

We laid it out on the bed and looked at it.

Did you ever meet her boyfriend? said Aggie.

What boyfriend? I said.

The boyfriend who hit her with his car, said Aggie.

What are you talking about? I said. I thought you said nobody ever talked to you about Katie.

I'm talking about her boyfriend who hit her with his car after their big fight, said Aggie. Mom said he couldn't see her in the snow or whatever. What are *you* talking about?

I put my hands over my eyes for a second trying to see something that wasn't there. Then I clasped my hands together so that my fingers met and formed a tiny pocket that held nothing. I looked at the wall and the gecko was gone. We had sunlight and traffic noise and breath. We had art. We had each other. We had ourselves. We had memories and we had lies. Those were the difficult-to-insure contents of our room.

What's your problem? said Aggie. Where's X.?

In the courtyard with Natalie, I said. In her playpen. Katie didn't have a boyfriend.

Yeah, she did, said Aggie. Mom told me.

Well, I said, no, she didn't have a boyfriend.

Well, said Aggie, whatever.

So, it couldn't have been the boyfriend who accidentally hit her with his car in a blizzard after a big fight, I said.

Who hit her then? said Aggie. She got up and went into the bathroom. I could see her reflection in the mirror. She was cleaning her belly button with a Q-tip soaked in sterilizing solution, dabbing it gently over and over, thoroughly.

Dad hit her, I said.

She stopped dabbing at her belly button.

She told him she was moving to Vancouver and he said she couldn't go and she said yeah I'm going, or something, and then she took off and was running down that road behind the second barn. I guess she was trying to get to the highway to hitchhike to the city and he took off after her in the truck and hit her.

She shouldn't have told him she was going, said Aggie.

I looked at her reflection. She had started dabbing at her belly button again, that little portal that connected her to her past. She kept dabbing while I talked so that eventually she had the cleanest belly button in all of Mexico.

Well, actually she didn't tell him that she was going, I said.

You just said she did, said Aggie.

I mean she did tell him that she was going, I said, but only after I told him.

You told Dad she was going to Vancouver? said Aggie. Why would you do that?

Because I didn't want her to go, I said.

You shouldn't have told him, said Aggie.

She was really excited about going, I said. I mean she was sad to be leaving but she was also really happy.

Uh-huh, said Aggie.

And it made me so mad, I said. That she was so happy about leaving. And she made me promise not to tell Dad.

So you promised you wouldn't? said Aggie.

Yeah, I said.

But then you did, said Aggie.

I know, I said. Yeah.

And then Dad went after her in his truck which is what you wanted him to do, said Aggie.

Yeah, I said, but to bring her home.

You shouldn't have told him, said Aggie.

And then he came home and told Mom he couldn't find her, I said. He put the truck in the garage and just waited around for a day or two for it to snow hard and then he told the cops that she had been upset about a fight with her boyfriend and had run off onto the road into the blizzard and still hadn't come home. So they went looking for her and found her body in the ditch. They said she had been hit by a car or a truck.

Dad said well, it must have been the boyfriend who hit her, and the cops said okay, who's her boyfriend and Dad said he had never met him and didn't know his name. He told the cops that Katie had been upset before she left and he had asked her what was wrong and she had said she and her boyfriend had had a fight. So then the cops said oh, okay, we'll ask around in the community. We'll talk to some of her friends to see if we can get some information and Dad said yes, thank you, that would be good. The cop asked Dad if he had a photograph of Katie and he said no. The cop said no photographs? And Dad said no again. He said our families don't have photographs.

A couple of days later the cops came back to our house and said that nobody in the community knew who her boyfriend was. Maybe it was a boy from the city, said Dad. And the cops said maybe. Then they said maybe it wasn't her boyfriend who hit her. And Dad said maybe not. He said maybe it was a trucker or a farmer in the area who had thought that he had hit a deer or a dog and had just kept going. Dad said the snow had been blinding that night and it would have been impossible for anyone to have seen her especially in the dark. The cops asked Mom and Dad some questions. They asked them why they thought Katie was running in the dark in a snowstorm wearing a light jean jacket and runners. Dad said she was upset about the fight with her boyfriend, he had already told them that. They said yes, but the fight must have happened earlier that day or even before that and why had she waited until so long after the fact to run off into the night. That didn't fit with their knowledge of human psychology and impulsive behaviour. Dad said well, he had thought that she had been talking to him over the phone that evening so the fight may have occurred over the phone immediately before she took off. The cops said well, they had contacted the Manitoba telephone system and there was no record of any phone activity that evening at all. None. Well, said Dad, the fight may have occurred earlier but Katie may have taken some time to work herself into a frenzy and then made the rash decision to run off into the night. Maybe, said the cop. Then he said that the autopsy had indicated that Katie's body had been in the ditch for longer than just that evening. Maybe two or even three days. Dad said that didn't make any sense at all and questioned the reliability of science. The cops asked Dad if maybe he had got the day wrong. They wondered if Katie had gone missing two or three days earlier, when the weather had been exceptionally clear and sunny and anybody driving down the road would have been able to have seen a running girl on the shoulder. Dad said no, he would have noticed if she'd been gone all that time, obviously. Then the cops were quiet for a second and asked Mom and Dad if they could talk to me alone.

Mom and Dad went outside into the yard and the cop asked me what kind of a girl Katie was. I said she was a fun girl. He asked me if she had had a boyfriend. I said yes. I was lying. The cop asked me if I knew who the boyfriend was. I said no, I had never met him. The cop said but she talked about him? I said yes, she did sometimes, not often. Then the cop made me tell him what she had said about her boyfriend and I said all she said was that he was funny and easygoing and made her laugh and liked her a lot. I didn't know what else to say. I didn't know anything about what boyfriends might be like. The cop asked me where he was from and I said I didn't know. Maybe the city. The cop asked me how Katie would have met a boy from the city when we were living so far away from it and she didn't have a driver's licence. I told the cop I didn't know. Then I thought of something and I told the cop that Katie had told me that her boyfriend had a really bad temper. That sometimes she'd say something or do something, anything, like tap the dashboard of his car with her foot, and he'd fly off the handle. He was really violent.

The cop said well, first he was funny and easygoing and now he's violent? I told the cop that he was both of those things, according to Katie. The cop asked me if she had ever called him by his name or had always spoken of him as her boyfriend this and her boyfriend that. I said yes, that she had never called him by his name. The cop said okay, can you tell me if there was any fighting between your dad and Katie? I said no, never. They asked me if any of the things she did ever made him angry and I said no, not at all. They asked me if I was sure about that. They said it was normal for fathers to sometimes become exasperated with their teenage daughters, to yell at them, or to forbid them from doing certain things. I didn't say anything. They asked me again if Katie had ever made Dad mad and I said no, never. Then the cops left and Mom and Dad came back into the kitchen. Mom went to take care of you and the boys, you were in the other room, and Dad asked me what

I had said to the cops. I told him and he said that was fine. Then the next day we were on our way to Mexico.

Aggie came out of the bathroom and took off her shirt. She put on a different one. Yeah, she said. That's when Mom told me about the boyfriend. When she came into the room where me and the boys were playing. She lied to me too. Then Aggie took that shirt off and put the other one back on. She took *Chocolate Mint Lip Gloss* and taped it to the wall beside the door. Then she walked out.

I found a blue emergency candle in the washroom cupboard and lit it and stuck it into an empty jar and brought it to the bed and set it there under Aggie's art. For the next hour or two I watched over Katie as she kicked out the walls around her. Finally around midnight or one in the morning Aggie came back and squeezed into bed next to me and Ximena and fell asleep in her clothes. In the morning I got up before she did. I got ready for work and then I woke her up for school.

After that Aggie painted a giant mural on brown paper and hung it over our bed. It was our family praying and holding hands around the table in our old kitchen in Canada. Katie's body was lying in the centre of the table and there were other regular dishes of food with spoons in them and steam coming up. All our eyes were closed except for our father's and he was staring straight at me. She painted a mural of a police lineup with three girls, herself, me and

Ximena, looking out at the camera, dirty and dishevelled and lost.

I asked Aggie if we could take those murals off the walls and put them in the closet. Why? she said. You don't want to be reminded of the fact that you're the daughter of a killer? I told her I was sorry for telling her the truth and she told me never to lie to her again.

ELEVEN

NOEHMI AND I WERE WORKING on the play. Well, all I really did was read my lines into a digital tape recorder over and over in different ways until she was happy with the way they sounded. I'll play yourself to you, she said. I listened to myself. I'm the memory of a doomed man, I thought. I couldn't save him. We sat in the darkness of the courtyard late at night after Aggie and Ximena and Natalie and Hubertus were asleep.

One more time, said Noehmi. Can you say it in a softer voice? Almost a whisper. Remember, your voice is being heard by a man dying of thirst and shame.

If you work hard, I whispered. If you want something badly enough. If you believe in yourself and never give up . . .

That's good, said Noehmi. But just try it with a bit more of a pause in between the sentences.

Okay, I said. If you work hard. If you want something badly enough. If you believe in yourself and never give up . . . I asked Noehmi if she thought it was true, what I was saying.

I don't know, she said. Do you?

I don't know, I said.

But it's the kind of thing a grade school teacher tells a kid, right? said Noehmi. It's a cliché and it's meant to be ironic in this context. Like, look where he is, right?

But he remembers it, I said.

Yeah, said Noehmi. For some reason it's one of the things he remembers.

Because he had a crush on her?

Yeah, said Noehmi. Sort of, that's a part of it. I don't know. She was just that person in his life who felt he had something to offer to the world.

When we were finished it was too late for Noehmi to go home so I got her a rollaway cot out of the shed and we hauled that upstairs to our room and she slept over and in the morning Natalie and Hubertus were so happy to see her that they made breakfast for all of us and I got to postpone going to work for a while. Dupont came to pick Noehmi up and I tried not to stare at them while they kissed. I tried not to notice how their lips met and opened and how they held each other close and casually in a loving embrace. They left and then Natalie asked me if I had noticed that Aggie seemed to be in a really bad mood.

Yeah, I said. She'll get over it. It's her age, I think.

Yeah, said Natalie. All those hormones.

Yeah, I said. And everything changing.

Yeah, said Natalie. Or not.

Yeah, I said.

Later that evening, when Aggie finally came home from school, which I think she was skipping with Israel these days mostly to hang out in Parque México with a pack of dogs, she told me that she was going to call the cops to tell them that our father was a murderer.

Aggie, I said. You are not.

Yeah, I am, she said. That's what normal people do.

What cops are you gonna call? I said. Cops in Chihuahua? In Canada?

Cops right here in D.F., she said.

They won't care, I said. They'll just laugh at you and tell you to stop bugging them.

Then in Chihuahua, said Aggie.

Same thing, I said. They won't believe you. Or even if they do they won't give a shit.

Fine, then in Canada, said Aggie.

Don't you think they already know? I said. Why would we have left for Mexico right after they came to talk to us if Dad didn't have something to hide?

So, she said. Now they can come and find him. We'll tell them where he is.

Aggie, I said, it doesn't work that way.

And then Mom and the boys can come and live with us in Mexico City and we can get a real house to live in instead of a hotel room.

It's not that simple, I said. The cops in Chihuahua would have to want to co-operate with the cops in Canada and they won't. They won't care and besides Dad has his own story.

You don't care about justice? said Aggie. You don't care about the truth? Don't you care about Katie? How do you know Dad isn't gonna kill someone else?

Well, I said. That's why we're fucking here! I didn't tell you the truth to make you all mad and do stupid things. I told you the truth because you had done up the room with the stars and the wind and I wanted to give you something in return. I told you the truth because I wanted you to stop hoping that Katie would somehow come back home and now I wish I hadn't.

I knew Katie wasn't going to come back home, said Aggie. Do you think I'm an idiot? Do you think I thought she could find us in the fucking desert?

Yeah, but that's not because we were lost, it's because she's dead! I said.

I know! said Aggie. I just thought maybe she wasn't. I thought maybe she was still in Vancouver.

Not *still* in Vancouver, I said. She never made it to fucking Vancouver!

Fine! said Aggie. Then just still alive, okay?

I know! I said. And that's why I wanted you to know the truth!

So okay, fine! said Aggie. Now I know the truth and I have to call the cops because that's what people do when they find out that someone has been murdered. Were you aware of that?

Do you know what would happen if you called the cops? I said. Then they'd know where you are and they'd be on Dad's side because he'd give them some money and they'd call you a mischief-making runaway and they'd take you and Ximena back home and that would be the end of it except for Dad beating the shit out of you and probably out of Mom for lying to him about Ximena being dead and I would never see you again and it wouldn't bring Katie back to life and you'd be dead inside forever! So, go ahead and make the call. Here, use my cell.

I threw my cellphone at her and missed. It hit the wall and a piece of it flew off and then the battery fell out of it. Ximena woke up and started laughing at us and jumping hard in her crib so that it rolled on its little wheels from one end of the room to the other. The people in the room below us banged on their ceiling. Aggie picked up the pieces of my phone and reassembled it and gave it back to me. I held it in my hand like an injured bird, tenderly. Aggie went and lifted Ximena out of her crib and changed her soaking diaper. I put my phone down on the bed and went into the bathroom to wash my face. I stood on the toilet and looked through the tiny barred window out at Mexico City. I couldn't see the end of it, the horizon where the sky met the earth, but I could remember clearly where it was. I could remember my father sobbing in the barn three days after we moved to Chihuahua. My mother had asked me to find him and tell him that supper was ready and I stood in the doorway of the barn and watched him cry, he was sitting on a bale and he had taken off his hat and he hadn't seen me in the darkness and then I cleared my throat and told him we were eating and he looked up at me and he said Irma, why did you tell me she was leaving? Why did you do that?

The next morning I was cleaning the big room on the second floor, the one that looked into the courtyard and not out towards the city, and I noticed an open newspaper lying on the floor beside the bed. There was a photograph of Diego Nolasco and the article was about the Mexico City premiere of his new movie *Campo Siete*. I looked at his picture and smiled hello, how are you? Then I ran upstairs to my room and got my notebook and ran back down and copied all the information. I folded the paper and put it on top of the little table by the window. It had never occurred to me that one day Diego's movie would be finished and available for the world to see. It hadn't occurred to me that all that energy, all that running around, all that waiting and all that anguish could result in one coherent song. I don't know why I thought of Diego's movie as a song. I had nothing else to compare it to, I guess, besides the Bible. The story hadn't made any sense to me, not really. It was all so chaotic and haphazard, like a dream with missing pieces, and rushed and then delayed and then right and then wrong and then broke and then euphoric and the skies weren't perfect and then they were and the real tears were fake and the fake tears were real and everyone was fighting and angry and having sex with each other and getting arrested and making threats and freezing at night and burning in the day and starving and stoned and exhausted and confused and sick and lonely and terrified. I wanted to see it. The idea alone of seeing *Campo Siete* obsessed and exhausted me.

I decided to see the movie by myself. I had thought about taking Aggie with me but I didn't want her to see Alfredo, her friend's dad, making pretend love to Marijke. I didn't want her to sit beside me moaning in agony or pretending to vomit. I also didn't know how the movie ended and I was afraid that maybe Oveja would be shot, or disappear somehow, and that Aggie would be devastated all over again. Then I thought about how angry she'd be with me if I didn't take her so I changed my mind and decided we'd go together and that the disturbing picture of a naked Alfredo or a wounded pit bull would be one that she would have to deal with on her own. I guess, at thirteen, there is almost nothing harder to bear than images of dead dogs and naked middle-aged men, but that's life.

I don't know how to describe the feeling of going to a movie. We went. Natalie and Hubertus agreed to babysit Ximena and even gave us extra money for popcorn. Aggie put on eyeliner. We took a bus to the theatre and paid for tickets and went inside and sat down in soft chairs and fought a little bit for the armrest in the middle (Aggie won) and waited in the dark. There were a lot of people. There was a lot of noise. And then it got very quiet and even darker and the curtain opened and the movie started. It was more exciting than anything I could remember happening, ever.

I still don't know what the movie is really about. I'm not smart enough. Or I don't want to know. I don't know. I cried all through the movie. I saw the skies and the cornfields and the faces of people I recognized. Even when Marijke said the lines that I had given her, the wrong ones, lines that were supposed to be funny, I cried. Diego had been right. It didn't really matter what words they used because all of their thoughts and feelings were being expressed in other more magical ways. Souls communicating with souls. It was amazing. I wish I could explain it. I wish I knew. There were dark circles under Marijke's eyes that I hadn't noticed before. She looked a little haunted. There was something about her I could see now, in her movie character, that I hadn't noticed in real life. For a second she stared directly into the camera and I thought no, no, Marijke, not directly into the camera. What did I tell you? Everything seemed to be out of place, the faces, the words, time. All the pictures strung together and people in them, walking, talking, kissing, dying. I felt so happy. Or maybe it wasn't happiness. There was something that I was beginning to understand but I didn't know what it was. It was like watching my own life. It was a pathway into myself. It was like the man dying in the duct in Noehmi's play as he hears the voices from his past. Maybe seeing a movie is like dying, but in a beautiful way. There are words that I want to say but they aren't strong enough to describe how I felt. Or they're too strong. And suffocating. Somewhere in the middle of those words is a word like, I don't know, peace or something. Harmony? That might be right, but probably not exactly.

So there we were. I cried quietly for everything that I had lost and for a few things that I had found and for reasons I couldn't explain and Aggie was I think trying hard not to giggle. We saw Oveja and she grabbed my arm and said he's alive! Which I thought was interesting in its way. In the way that it might not actually be true but that it seemed true in that very moment. I saw myself lying under a tree with my back to the camera. Diego had used me as a body double for Marijke who had refused to do that scene because of the snakes. It was amazing. I had never seen a photo of myself, let alone a moving picture. I saw Marijke's giant face fill every inch of the screen. I almost screamed. When we saw the kids from our campo Aggie said ha! Look! It's Aughte! And somebody behind us told her to be quiet. The fields and the skies were so empty and lonely and alluring. I asked Aggie in a whisper if it made her want to go home and she said no in a loud voice and was told again to shut up. The movie ended and we stretched our legs out and got ready to leave but then the lights came on and a woman with a microphone walked up to the front of the theatre and onto the stage and said that tonight was a very special night because Diego Nolasco was with us and would now be answering questions from the audience.

I didn't know what to do. I didn't want Diego to see us and tell someone, anyone, the police, our father, where we were. But the lights were on and if we stood up now and tried to leave we'd be completely conspicuous and I imagined

Diego calling out hello Irma and Aggie, *cómo están*? So I hunkered down a bit in my seat and told Aggie we'd stay for the questions and then leave.

Can I ask one? said Aggie.

No! I said.

The woman behind us had clearly been tested. My God, she said, have you no respect?

I'm sorry, I said. We do, we do. I'm sorry.

Aggie turned around to say something to the woman and I dug my fingers into her leg and whispered in Low German that she should just shut up and stay calm and then the woman started to say something about how Aggie was a kid, a punk, and shouldn't be there and I thought about agreeing with her but then Diego's voice was everywhere and he was up there on the stage in nice clothes and talking into the microphone and smiling and there was applause, a lot of it, that drowned us all out and Aggie settled back into her chair and the woman did too and we all more or less listened to what he had to say.

Audience member: How did the Mennonites feel
about a movie being made about them?
Diego: There was some interference, certainly.
There was some resistance initially. But
eventually they realized that we were there
to make a respectful film which I think
you would agree with, having seen it now.
Alfredo, who plays the husband, was very
co-operative and helped smooth things out
for everyone. For the most part the

Mennonites were happy to have us there and were very generous with their time and their land and homes, locations where we shot.

Audience member: Had you considered opening the film in Chihuahua, where the Mennonites might have seen it?

Diego: I had, yes, and I still want to bring it to the community so that they can see it, but the logistics of that, now, are still . . . complicated.

Audience member: The film is stunning. It's awe-inspiring. Thank you for making it. My question is, what was the shoot like? What were some of the difficulties you encountered?

Diego: Thanks. Um, thanks a lot. Well, we had to wait for the right weather, often. It was the rainy season when we were shooting, it was supposed to be, but the rain didn't come when it was supposed to so we had to use artificial rain. That was problematic but it worked eventually. There also, it was often very hot, and in fact we lost . . . or one of our lead actors went missing for several days because . . . she had heatstroke and went missing in the desert. She walked away from the shoot and got lost. We had warned her not to walk but . . . Originally I had a girl from the community that I had hired as a translator and sort of companion but she was . . . she wasn't able to stay so . . . But . . . anyway . . . the actress was okay in the end. She had to be hospitalized for exhaustion or . . . for several days so during that time we shot other scenes.

Audience member: Hello Diego. I want to first of all congratulate you. In my opinion *Campo Siete* is a masterpiece. You are an extraordinary artist. You've transformed a place of austerity and poverty into a place of strange beauty. I don't know how you do it but I think I can say for everyone here tonight that we are all so grateful that you *do* do it. Congratulations. Bravo.

Diego: Oh, well, thanks very much.

Audience member: Why did you choose to make a movie about Mennonites?

Diego: I don't care about the Mennonites as a group. Not at all. I'm interested in the fact that nobody would understand their language and that they were uniform. There's no distinction, one from the other, and so they are props, essentially, for pure emotion. Even their setting, you don't know what era it is or where, blonds in Mexico, it doesn't matter, ultimately, when all you want is to communicate an emotional truth.

Audience member: I read something in one of the papers here months ago that there had been a violent incident at the campo where you were making the film. Can you speak of that?

Diego: Yes, there was a shooting.

Audience member: Did it involve your crew or any people involved in the making of the film?

Diego: No. No, no, it was . . . there was a shooting at the farm down the road.

Audience member: In the paper it said that the shooting was drug related. I found that so surprising, that the Mennonites would be involved in that type of thing.

Diego: Yes, well . . . it is, I guess. I don't know the details. I believe it was a debt of some kind.

Audience member: A drug debt?

Diego: Yeah . . . I think so. The guy who lived there was just . . . he just stored the drugs for . . . I don't know who. It's a very remote area so it's a good place for that. The people are very poor. There were . . . there aren't many opportunities. And apparently the person came to get the . . . to get it . . . and it wasn't there and he became very angry and killed the . . . guy.

Audience member: In the paper it mentioned, I think, that the victim was related to a member of your crew.

Diego: Member of my crew? No, no, I don't think . . . oh, yeah, well . . . the person I was talking about before, the girl I had hired as a translator for Marijke . . . that person . . . the victim . . . or . . . he was her relative.

Audience member: He was her father?

Diego: He was her husband.

Audience member: I understand you used natural lighting in the making of your film. I'm curious about how that worked for interior shots.

Diego: I'm sorry?

Audience member: I understand you used natural lighting in the making of your film. How did you manage to get enough light for the interior shots?

Diego: If there's not a lot of natural light coming in from windows or with one or two lamps, then that's how it is. The shot is dark. *(He turns to the woman who introduced him, indicating that he'd like the question-and-answer period to be over.)*

Woman: We only have time for one or two more questions. Yes?

Audience member: Are you in the process of working on something new? Are you writing another script?

Diego: Yes, of course. I'm always working on something new.

Audience member: Can you tell us what it's about?

Diego: It's not about Mennonites, that much I'll say. *(The audience laughs and Diego smiles and waves goodbye.)*

Audience member: Is it—

Woman: I'm sorry, we'll have to stop there. Thank you, Diego, for— *(The audience bursts into applause and drowns out the woman and Diego waves again and leaves the stage.)*

Aggie and I left the theatre and walked into a park across the street. It was very dark for Mexico City. We sat down on a small wooden bench and Aggie whispered things to me, the consolation of a thirteen-year-old. He came back! she said, beautiful words and sweet promises and hugs, while I wept. Aggie didn't loosen her grip, though. Then later, at home, after she had fallen asleep with streaks of eyeliner on her face and Ximena had polished off her bottle and flung it at the wall, I took my notebook out and wrote a list of the sins I had committed. It's good to have an itinerary even if it only leads to hell.

I broke a promise and told my father the truth, that Katie was planning to go to Vancouver, because I didn't want her to leave and because of that she ended up dead.

I lied to the police about everything because I didn't want my dad to go to jail and because of that we had to move to Mexico where the life gradually drained out of my mother.

By lying to the police I killed my soul and stopped believing in an afterlife because life after death seemed almost exactly the same as life before it.

I selfishly took a job as a translator which resulted in Aggie being curious about filmmaking and late nights and boys which resulted in her being beaten by our father.

I stole Jorge's drugs to sell for money to run away from home and buy plane tickets with my little sisters so we wouldn't end up being killed by my father. (I also took Diego's truck for a while, which constituted more stealing.)
By stealing Jorge's drugs to sell to Carlito Wiebe to save myself Jorge ended up dead.
I killed my sister.
I killed my mother.
I killed my husband.
I killed my soul.

I read over my sins. I hit myself on the side of my head. I pressed my hands into my face. I tried to push back. I walked into the bathroom and looked at myself in the mirror. I saw the red outlines of ten fingers on my face. I picked up the bottle that Ximena had thrown away and put it in the sink. I walked back into the bedroom and looked at my sleeping sisters. I remembered Jorge's foaming shoes. How he waited on that corner. His shame. My shame. I didn't know what to do. I wondered if this was how it always was when you realize big things, for instance, that you're a serial murderer, that all you can do is go into different rooms and look at things and people and not understand. Marijke had been wrong. What's terrible is not easy to endure and what's good is not easy to get. Why had she looked so haunted in the movie? I don't know. I touched the spot between my eyes, the source of my internal light and cosmic energy. I waited for something to happen but nothing did. I knelt beside the bed and covered my face again with my hands and prayed for forgiveness. Please God, I said. Help me to live. When I opened my eyes nothing had changed. I closed them again and again. I remembered Marijke telling me that she had done that too, in the desert, hoping that the next time she opened her eyes she'd see her son. And then I remembered that she had never told me why she'd stopped aging at fourteen. I closed my eyes and tried to see Jorge. I opened them again and went back into the bathroom and sat on the edge of the tub and washed my feet thoroughly and then dried them very carefully, between each toe, all over. I went to bed. I dreamed that I was standing in the front yard of my house in Canada and waving goodbye to everyone I loved. I had to go away, I didn't know where, and the sun was shining beautifully and my grandma and my parents and my brothers and sisters and Jorge and all my friends from school were standing on the front steps and smiling and waving and telling me they loved me. Maybe they were crying a little bit but they were also trying to look happy and positive. And in that moment it was too much, I felt all the love, more than I had ever felt before in my life, a universal love, and I didn't want to go after all. But in my dream I had to go. I didn't know why.

After that day I developed a headache that wouldn't go away. I saw lightning flashes in the corners of my eyes like two storms coming in slowly from both the east and the west. Aggie bought me a giant bottle of Tylenol and I popped them all day long while I tried to get my work done. Natalie said that it might be because of the changing season, it was spring and the jacarandas were exploding, or it might be allergies or it might be stress. Or it might be a brain tumour, said Aggie, pressing down on my optical nerve. It's just storms, I'd say. I don't know.

Do you hear thunder? said Aggie. Do you feel the wind picking up in your brain? She threw the giant bottle of Tylenol at me and I shook them straight out of the bottle into my mouth without using water to wash them down. Hubertus got me a bunch of vitamins and minerals and cod liver oil too, but none of that stuff worked at all. He told me not to work for a few days and lie in the dark with a cold cloth on my forehead so I tried doing that but lying around all day just made me restless and nervous. Aggie stayed home from school to take care of Ximena so I could rest but that wasn't really working either because X. liked to crawl all over me and suck on the wet washcloth and Aggie was getting bored and pissed off. She wanted to go to school and she wanted to see Israel and get on with her regular life.

I'm trying to work something out, I told her.

What are you trying to work out?

I don't know, I said.

That's why the storms?

Do you study English in school? I asked her.

Israel's mom thinks you should talk to a priest.

I'm not Catholic, I said.

She said it doesn't matter, said Aggie. You get to hear him say my daughter.

Say my daughter?

He has to call you my daughter, she said. It's just how they talk.

You went? I said.

Yeah, I go sometimes with Israel. His mom makes him.

Really? I said.

So the next day I asked Natalie if she could watch X. for an hour or so while I went to church and she said sure and I found a church and walked into a confession booth. I waited for the priest to call me his daughter but he didn't. He waited for me to speak, to confess something, and I wanted to tell him all about the lies and the stealing and the murders but I couldn't speak. I didn't want to tell him anything because I was still afraid that if I did, something bad would happen to my father. I was silent. The priest asked me if I was going to talk to him and I said no. Then after a little while he told me that he had quite a lot of people to talk to that day. I didn't say anything. He said so if I wanted to come back another time that would be okay with him but that he should probably make himself available for other people now. He said it kindly. He apologized for his awkwardness. I waited for him to say my daughter. I didn't say anything. He asked me again if I would prefer to come back another time and I still didn't say anything and then he said please, my daughter, I honestly don't know what to tell you.

I was back in my bed with lightning raining down on my cerebral cortex and Ximena's screams drifting up from the courtyard. I was still trying to form a picture of Jorge in my mind. I saw Katie getting ready to leave, stuffing clothes into a backpack and begging me to promise not to tell. I saw my father as a little boy on a road in Russia. I was trying to get to the bottom of things. I was trying to formulate a thought. Or a cure. Even a cure that had only one part would be enough for now. Aggie was walking around with Ximena trying to get her to calm down after she bit into a live electrical cord. She was singing to her, a silly little Low German song about ducks swimming in the sea. It was a new kind of scream for Ximena. She was in real pain. She had suffered a serious shock. I was familiar with her entire repertoire of screams and what they meant but this was something much different. She was surprised and hurt. She was fragile after all, a helpless baby. I listened to her screams and then I put the pillow over my head but I could still hear them. And then, because my little sister had bit into an electrical cord and would not be consoled, or something, I'm not sure why, really, the gathering storms in my head disappeared and I had figured out the solution to my own problem. I understood what it was to want someone to stay. And I knew what to do next. And I knew the answer to my own question: if this was the last day of your life what kind of a story would you write?

YOU MUST BE PREPARED TO DIE!

I read over the original heading in my notebook, the one that Diego had given me a long time ago to record my thoughts and observations. I pondered his dark advice. I scratched out the word DIE and wrote LIVE. Then that seemed cheesy and too uncooly emphatic so I added the words SORT OF. AT LEAST TRY. Even that seemed bossy so I added, in parentheses, a joke: OR DIE TRYING. Then I told myself that it wasn't funny and crossed it all, every word of it, out and started again.

I'm on a plane to Chihuahua city. I have a photograph for my mother that she will have to hide and only look at while my father's in the field. It's of the three of us, her Mexico City girls. Aggie has a pierced eyebrow now and the craziest smile and most beautiful eyes and Ximena is struggling to get out of my arms so that she can assault the photographer (Noehmi). I'm holding on to her and saying something. My mouth is half open and my eyebrows are furrowed, like always.

Natalie and Hubertus gave me the money for a ticket and said all they wanted in return was for me to promise to come back. Aggie didn't want to come with me which is good because I didn't want her to either. She's young enough that my father could force her to stay at home and I didn't want to go through that again. Aggie wants to go see thousands of naked people in the Zócalo having their picture taken. Noehmi is on her spring break from university so she's going to take care of Ximena (whom she has started calling Cricket) so that Aggie can still go to school while I'm gone and Natalie's friend Fernande is going to do my job for me for the few days that I'm away because she needs extra money to pay her divorce lawyer. Ximena can't come, obviously, because she's not even supposed to be alive. This time, if my father asks me where my sister is, I'll ask him the same question.

I'm on the plane. I don't know what to write. Should I write down my dreams?

The time is 11:02 a.m. My name is Irma Voth. I'm on a plane. I'm not a good person. I'm not a smart person. I might be a free person. If this is how it feels.

I scratched that out because there were only parts of it I thought were true and closed my notebook and looked out the window at air. I opened my notebook again thinking that I had all sorts of ideas and things to write about but now I'm not sure. I heard my mother's voice. Irma, she said, just begin.

I want to be forgiven. I want to be forgiven for causing the deaths of so many people I've loved. I feel like that might never happen. I don't know how it will happen or if it will happen. I don't think it will but I want it to. I don't feel forgiven by God. I want to be forgiven by the people I love. Wilson told me that art is redemptive. My father told me that art is a lie. I can't forgive myself but I can forgive my father. And my hope is that we'll both be brought back to life.

I rented a small red car at the airport in Chihuahua city and drove the twisty desert mountain road to Cuauhtémoc and then I drove the flat, hot highway home to Campo 6.5.

I drove past Carlito's rundown house and Alfredo's well-kept farm with plastic flowers in the planters and past the crashed crop-duster where I'd asked Jorge to meet me for the first time. I saw a cow with his hoof stuck in the runner bars that were there to prevent him from escaping. I knew from experience not to try to help him because he'd be violent and enraged. I drove past the filmmakers' old house which had been my cousins' old house. I felt the tender touch of Wilson's dying hand on my body, on every part of it, and heard him call me beautiful. Are you still alive? I said.

The house that Jorge and I had lived in was missing. There was black grass where it had been. That's all. No sheds either. Nothing. Jorge, I said. I'm so sorry. I pictured us in a lighthouse in the Yucatán, slow dancing in a round room, looking out towards the Caribbean Sea.

I kept driving. I saw my little brothers playing with a dead snake or something on the driveway and my mother leaning against the fence like she'd been out there for a long time, weeks, maybe months, just waiting for me to show up. I got out of the car and waved to her and started walking towards her and then she began to run. She was running and laughing. She was running and laughing! And then we were hugging each other so hard, my God, she was strong. She wouldn't let me go. My brothers joined us in this wild, joyful embrace and then I saw my father coming out of the house, using his hand to shade the sun from his eyes, and he also came towards us, not running and laughing but walking firmly and steadily. And I remembered a few sentences from *Jakob von Gunten*, which the bookseller in the park had given me:

And one day I would be a beggar and the sun would be shining and I would be so happy, and I wouldn't ever want to know why. And then Mamma would come and hug me—what nice imaginings these are!

And then I parked the car and walked towards my old house. The curtains were closed and it was late in the day, stars were everywhere, and I could hear the incomprehensible noises of different animals attempting to communicate with each other in the dark and the voices of my brothers and my parents singing some old ancient song in Low German and I stood outside the door for a while and listened before I went inside to say hello, how are you?

ACKNOWLEDGEMENTS

For their tremendous efforts in the making of this book I'd like to thank Sarah Chalfant, Michael Schellenberg, Hannah Griffiths, Louise Dennys, Marion Garner, Kelly Hill, Deirdre Molina, José Molina and Nicola Makoway.

On page 175 I quoted from a beautifully written obituary sent to me in a letter from a friend. I know that it ran in the *Globe and Mail* newspaper but regret that I have no idea when and do not know who was being so well celebrated.

Many thanks to Neal Rempel for kindly giving me permission to use some of the details of his play *The Last Words of Duct Schultz* for my own purposes in the book, beginning on page 214.

MIRIAM TOWES was born in the small Mennonite town of Steinbach, Manitoba. She has published five novels and a memoir of her father, and is the recipient of numerous literary awards in Canada, including the Governor General's Literary Award (for *A Complicated Kindness*) and the Rogers Writers' Trust Fiction Prize (for *The Flying Troutmans*). In 2010 she received the prestigious Writers' Trust Engel/Findley Award for her body of work. *Irma Voth* is Toews's most recent novel. She lives in Toronto.